Awesomesauce:

the musical*

*book may not contain any actual musical numbers

Special Thanks to:

The very patient crew at Wanderer's Refuge,

Mikhail Bulgakov,

the Sovereign Overlord,

Karen Browning,

Marc Fernandes,

my incredible wife,

and my amazing son.

This book is dedicated to the three greatest surrogate moms a kid with a dead mom could ask for:

Karin Jones,

Gail Fernandes,

and,

Judy Dommermuth

Thank you.

"Fame is a four letter word"

- someone you've never heard of

Today

Chapter One

Wherein Thomas explores the viscosity of bodily fluids.

Thomas Sourwood looked down at the tile of the men's room floor of the West Encino Community Center. That is the one thing no one ever tells you about the San Fernando Valley, thought Thomas, they never mention the dust. Folks came from all over the world to see the San Fernando Valley. They came from places where they felt they have a fine grasp on dust, but until you've tried to clean dust off anything in the Valley, you just don't understand.

Thomas thought that it had something to do with the natural desert ecosystem affected by low-lying smog from the surrounding freeways, creating a kind of "super dust," which at times is so thick and dry that it can be as slippery as ice. The slightest bit of moisture would quickly turn the dust into a thick, inky goo, which would cling to everything, including, but not limited to, most cleaning supplies.

The amount of dust on this bathroom floor was remarkable. It wasn't going to be easy to clean. The blood wasn't going to help.

It pooled underneath Dr. Orga's head, then spread from there and mixed with the dust. The dust slowed its spread across the floor, darkened its hue, and increased its viscosity, causing it to become a kind of gelatinous slime, which crept slowly toward Thomas's beige high-tops.

"Dr. Orga?" said a soft voice, as the industrial green bathroom door slowly opened. Thomas recognized the woman as the Doctor's personal assistant. It bothered him that he couldn't remember her name. He would have asked, but she seemed occupied, screaming hysterically as she stared at the body on the floor.

Thomas thought that it was rather interesting that even though Dr. Orga had been reduced to leading his self-help programs at a place like the West Encino Community Center, that he could still afford an assistant, especially one as attractive as the one who was now screaming for someone to call 911.

As Thomas ran from the bathroom, he was quick to admonish himself. The thought that an attractive assistant would somehow cost more than one who wasn't was horribly misogynistic. Thomas wasn't usually prone to those tendencies. He prided himself on his open-mindedness and fierce sense of equality. He had almost lost his job as a TSA agent for refusing to give closer scrutiny to flyers of Arab descent.

He shoved his way past the large crowd that was beginning to clog the beige aisle, curious to find out what was happening in the men's room. Loud, dated, inspirational music was playing. The large photograph of Dr. Orga and the cover of his new book, "Yes to Change! Empowering Your Empowerment! Available in the lobby of this theatre," smiled warmly from the stage.

Thomas walked calmly out to the expansive parking lot. He didn't start to run until the attractive assistant screamed that he should be stopped. It was a high, shrill, "Someone stop that man!" It was a voice that was screaming out of fear rather than authority.

Thomas scrambled into his car, and left the parking lot. The newly paved lot, his under inflated tires, and the dust, caused the wheels to squeal and spin, creating the illusion that he was peeling out at a high rate of speed. As he drove from the parking lot of the West Encino Community Center and into the parking lot of the neighboring strip mall, at eleven miles an hour, he could hear people wondering if anyone had called 911, or if they could remember the license plate of the car that was slowly getting away?

Thomas reached into his pocket and pulled out his electronic cigarette. He took a long drag. Thomas hit the speed bump harder than he had meant to, causing his electronic cigarette to bounce from his hand and onto the floor of the car. Thomas frantically reached down to pick it up. As he did his foot jammed down on the gas pedal. After a few moments of frantically searching, Thomas giggled to himself. The electronic cigarette wasn't a real cigarette. It wouldn't ignite anything. He looked up in time to see the wheelchair, a quick moment before he struck it with his car. The chair and its occupant both flew high into the air landing behind the car with a sickening crunch.

Thomas thought that if he had been given time to process his first manslaughter, he may have reacted to his second. He wondered if it would have been less of a shock, or more. He wondered if he would have cried, mourning the second poor unfortunate soul he had mistakenly killed. Or, would he laugh uncontrollably? Sadly, Thomas would never be able to experience his second manslaughter ever again.

Thomas's car bottomed out after hitting another speed bump. Sparks flew as he fishtailed up Ventura Boulevard.

Eighteen Months Ago

Chapter Two

Wherein Bruce reads a book.

The Brisbane Whalers had never truly been in contention for the Premiership Cup this season. But, considering the amount of press the Australian Rules Football club had received since signing star player Bruce Prise, it seemed as though they had a chance. Fans refer to many popular players as "Rock Stars." Star footballer Bruce Prise actually was one, or would be as soon as his hit album was released in the United States.

Most of his fellow Australians thought of him as a national treasure. His relaxed attitude and humility helped tremendously. If the superstar athlete and music phenom had been a bit more like his American counterparts, then his countrymen would easily have mocked him, or at the very least ignored him, rather than propelling him to stardom.

He had been voted most eligible bachelor in the AFL as well as Sexiest Aussie for three consecutive years. When he wasn't training or performing his music in front of thousands of fans, he would appear on the talk show circuit, where he was a perennial favorite. Whether it was a cooking segment, or trying to keep a straight face while being interviewed by a crowd of primary school children, he was endlessly charming, nice to his fans, and respectful of women. He drank, but rarely to excess, and when he did, he was just more affable than usual. Bruce Prise's only real flaw was a crippling fear of flying.

"You know what you should do," said his Brazilian supermodel girlfriend in her strange German-accented English, "just relax and read a book."

"Read a bloody book?" said Bruce, through the door to the cavernous master bathroom. Bruce was seated on the marble Italian tile, in a corner, his entire body shaking. The large claw foot tub, which had been rescued from the demolition of a world-renowned Parisian hotel and restored at great expense, was full of tepid water. Bruce had walked into the bathroom with every intention of taking a nice relaxing bath.

Earlier, as he stared at the tub filling, all he could imagine was how long his flight to Los Angeles would be over nothing but water. Suspended, by virtue of Bernoulli's principle, thirty-thousand feet over the abyss that is the Pacific Ocean. Then, he imagined the myriad ways he could drown.

First, there was the plane crashing into the ocean, the impact killing most of the people on board, leaving him to struggle in vain until he slowly succumbed to exhaustion, and cold salty death filling his lungs.

Second, there was the possibility of a terrorists' bomb going off, killing most of the people on board, but leading him to plummet towards the Pacific. He would, of course, somehow survive diving into the ocean, but be pulled so far under due to his velocity, that as he struggled to reach the surface of the water, he would succumb to exhaustion, just a few meters away from the surface, the cold salty death filling his lungs.

Third, the plane could plummet into the ocean, its fuselage staying intact, but slowly slipping into the depths of the Pacific Ocean. Many people would die simply due to the panic, but as the pressurized cabin sinks lower and lower, eventually the windows crack. The water would rush in killing most of the people on board. He would survive by locking himself in the first class bathroom. The water would slowly begin to rise until finally his lungs would fill with cold salty death.

Once he reached thirty-seven possible ways to die, he turned off the water and curled up on the floor and quietly rocked himself.

"Read a bloody book!" screamed Bruce through the door. "I have a medicine cabinet full of pills to help me relax. Not one of them fucking works!"

"You do realize," said the supermodel, "that all of this silliness is just in your head, don't you?"

"Of course I do," said Bruce. "And I've got the fucking therapist bills to prove it."

"So, when you get to the airport, grab the first book that catches your eye," she said. "Pour yourself into it, forget that you're even on a plane."

"It's not that easy," said Bruce. "This is very difficult for me!"

"Of course it is, sweetheart," she said. "But, I'm certain that you can do it. When you get back, we'll go somewhere special."

"What the fuck is wrong with you?" he said. "Don't you remember! Don't plan anything big! If you plan something big, it will be like in those disaster movies from the seventies! Fuck! Now I know I'm going to fucking die!"

"You're not going to die, Bruce," she said. "You're just flying to America. Your ride is here."

Bruce thought about how he could miss his flight. Then he remembered; he and his assistant had planned on his panic attack, thus the reason why the limo was arriving a full eight hours before his flight was scheduled to leave, giving his assistant enough time to remove the locked bathroom door from its hinges. Then Bruce lead his assistant on a naked chase through his house and out onto the grounds while his manager finished packing for him.

Bruce was hogtied and thrown into the back of the waiting limo. Bruce was too busy screaming obscenities to notice his manager pulling the tablet out of its case. He swiped to the correct program and then propped it up in front of Bruce's face.

The screen blinked and then showed Bruce's smiling face. "Now," said the Bruce on the screen to the Bruce in the back of the limo, "if I'm not mistaken you're probably hogtied and in the back of a limo on your way to the airport to catch a flight to America. I know you don't want to go right now, but talking to you, as you, from a few weeks ago, trust me. You need to do this. You're going to be a guest on Mr. Willet's late night talk show to promote the album. You're going to play a few songs and be genuinely charming,

something that I know you do very well. I
know that there isn't a whole lot that I can
tell you that is actually going to get you to
calm down. But, I have heard the idea of
pouring yourself into a book might be fun."

"Fuck you!" screamed the Bruce in the
limo.

"Look," said the Bruce on the tablet.
"Mr. Willet is the self-proclaimed king of late
night; the boundaries he's pushing with his
comedy are genius! I mean, this guy is
brilliant! You cannot pass this up!"

When they arrived at the airport, a
wheelchair was sent for Bruce. He was
placed in it and rushed toward the first class
lounge.

"Wait!" he screamed, as he passed a
bookstore. "No, really! I want to buy a book."

Bruce's manager stopped pushing the
wheelchair.

"Are you serious?" said the manager.

"Totally, no tricks," said Bruce. "The
bookstore, just back there! She said I should
grab the first one that caught my eye."

"Which one?" said his assistant.

"The one with the boots on it."

Bruce's assistant walked back to the bookstore, while his manager stayed with Bruce. The assistant spied the lone copy of a book whose provenance was really unique.

The cover of Crazy Rhythm had a lone pair of combat boots sitting in a snowdrift. Crazy Rhythm had been written by an obscure, American, independent author by the name of Nicolas Irons. He had self-published the book after a long and frustrating time of attempting to get a reputable publisher to read it. It was available in the United States through a few print-on-demand platforms as well as an e-book. It was the e-book that was originally pirated, and translated into Chinese.

It's a bizarre love story between a blind German woman and a Jewish man, whose escape from a concentration camp and impersonation of an American soldier have him weaving a web of deceit to both keep himself, as well as the young woman he is falling in love with, alive. The novella itself was passable, but in spite of its pulpy melodramatic prose, no attention to historical detail, and lack of an ending, it somehow struck a chord with many people for singles day. Crazy Rhythm was the number one best seller in China for six months. Nicolas never made a dime. The publishing house behind the pirated copy quickly planned on publishing this obscure novella through South East Asia, offering other translations of the book.

Leading the translation of the book into English, they hired a cunning Japanese linguist. The linguist, never being a very big fan of the publishing house, nor of the idea of pirated material, instead of translating the book, simply ordered a copy of the original e-book from a reputable American website. Without changing a single line, she simply submitted it to the publishing house.

The publishing house, impressed with the speed with which she was able to translate the text, offered her a substantial bonus. No one at the publishing house bothered to notice that she included the title page, which had all of the original copyright information. Nearly ten thousand copies of the English translation of <u>Crazy Rhythm</u> were printed and placed on a boat to Australia.

However, during the long voyage across the South Pacific, the United States and China signed a new trade agreement. It included some very strong language condemning the violation of international copyrights. In a very public display of support for the new agreement, the Chinese government arrested everyone at the publishing house.

With everyone from publishing house in prison, there was no one to ensure the shipment of books were claimed. They sat in a warehouse in Brisbane, where, due to a paperwork snafu, they were purchased as part of a real estate auction by a woman who owned a chain of independent book stores. After she discovered the books, she put them on sale in all of her stores, which, as fate would have it, included the one that Bruce Prise passed in the Brisbane airport.

Three hours into the flight when Bruce

had exhausted his different drug options, the jumbo jet hit what might be described as mild turbulence. Bruce, in his heightened state, was convinced that the turbulence was either due to a bomb going off, or the fact that they were flying into the eye of a typhoon. He tried to hit the button to call the airline steward back to his private, first class suite on the plane. Unfortunately, by this time the airline stewards we so tired of dealing with Mr. Prise, Bruce had to deal with it on his own. His shaky hand, dripping with sweat, slowly pulled out the copy of Crazy Rhythm. He took a deep breath and opened the book to the first page.

Chapter Three

An excerpt from <u>Crazy Rhythm</u> by Nicolas Irons

Anton stopped at the tree line. The large open field before him had no cover. One lone tree interrupted the blanket of new snow. There weren't any tracks. Anton had been clear of trails and roads for days. He stayed deep in the wood, following the sun west. He kept losing it in the clouds, but kept moving, even when he thought he was walking in circles. This clearing was the first he had seen. The clearing meant progress. It was something new. But, leaving the shelter of the trees would leave him exposed.

Besides, he thought, my feet have finally gone numb. I could just sit down here in the mud and wait. The mud would be warmer than the snow. With my luck, walking through the snow would somehow wake them up, and they would start hurting again.

The snow became heavier. It pelted the snow on the field with a sharp sound like hail hitting a sidewalk. That settled it, thought Anton. I'm not going out there. Then he saw it.

The wind began to howl. Something hidden just behind the lone tree swung into view, something hanging from the tree. At this distance, he couldn't be certain what. Anton began fantasizing.

What it could be?

The hollow feeling in his belly immediately caused him to imagine it was food. This drew him out from the tree line.

"Why would anyone hang their food from a tree like that?" Anton imagined his wife saying.

He stopped to think.

It was a good question.

His wife always asked good questions.

"Bears," said Anton.

"Bears?" he could hear her more clearly now. "That is just like you. Getting your hopes up."

"Don't bring up the telegram," said Anton.

"Of course I'm going to bring up the telegram," she said.

"When had we ever received a telegram?" said Anton. "And from Uncle Hans? Do you remember visiting him in Bremen? The way the food kept coming?"

"Again with you and your stomach!" she said. "I want you to think about this."

"Where else is there to go?" said Anton.

"I hate it when you get your hopes up like this," she said.

Anton turned to see her sitting at the kitchen table, next to the stove. The sepia wallpaper in the small apartment had once been bright yellow. The soot from the street and time had faded it and turned it into the forgettable hue it was today. Anton closed his eyes. When he opened them he was standing in front of a train station.

The train station was grimmer than usual. The low, grey fog trapped the soot and smoke, muting all the colors. Anton wore his best suit. He hadn't cared that it had holes in the elbows, Uncle Hans wouldn't notice them. He would be too busy with the girls. That was the way he had always been, no matter how fat he became. It seemed the bigger Hans got, the more full of life and affable he became. Hans had had a successful stage career for most of the twenties. This, he quickly translated into a successful film career. But, his success quickly went to his waistline. That was the way it had always been for anyone on Anton's side of the family. Just the slightest bit of quality in either food or drink, would end up going straight to their bellies. The last time Anton and his wife went to visit Hans at his summer home in Bremen, she had put Anton on a diet as soon as they were back.

A small group of soldiers walked by. Anton faded into the background. Not that he had done anything wrong, but he didn't want Uncle Hans to get the wrong impression, or deal with the hassle.

Then, a crowd came from the platform, from what must have been Hans' train. It had been a long time since Anton had been to the train station. When he was younger, his grandmother would take him to the train station when she was picking someone up and he would see the swarm of smiling people on holiday. Some seemed exotic, and they were happy to finally reach a destination. Even those who had traveled in the worst seats were happy to get up and walk around, waking their tired legs and bruised behinds.

This was different. Everyone getting off the

train was gray. Their skin, their clothes, their whole demeanor was gray. Anton's heart sank, until he saw Uncle Hans. There he was with a broad smile on his face as he caught Anton's eye. Hans had the same gray pallor as everyone else, and he was very thin, the thinnest Anton could ever remember him, but his eyes were dancing.

"Anton!" he bellowed as he walked toward him. They met in a strong embrace and Anton was surprised how thin Hans really was, the baggy clothes making him seem healthier than he was.

"Uncle, it is wonderful to see you," said Anton. "Where are your bags?"

"None of that this trip, Anton," said Hans. "We're traveling a bit lighter than usual."

"I can see that," said Anton.

"Did you bring a car?" said Hans.

"No," said Anton. "Sadly, we've lost the car."

"Lost?" said Hans. "Or did they take it?"

"No matter," said Anton. "It is a quick walk to the hotels off the square."

"Yes, about that, Anton," said Hans.

The group of soldiers was returning, and was beginning to force people off the platform.

"We should go," said Anton.

"Agreed," said Hans. "Take me to see your beautiful wife."

"The apartment?"

"Yes," said Hans. "Please."

Anton stared deep into his hollow face, and it faded into snow. Anton looked around at the snowy field.

"It didn't seem fair at all," said his wife's voice. "Not in the slightest!"

"Still we made the most of it, didn't we?" said Anton.

He waited to hear her again. It had been so long since he had, he had almost forgot how sweet she sounded even when she was scolding him.

Chapter Four

Wherein Bruce meets a TSA agent.

Bruce stood before the TSA and customs agent. His shirt was stuck to him, covered in sweat and vomit. His hair was matted to one side. His eyes were wild.

Bruce's manager looked at the two officials and tried to hide his nervous energy. He looked at the badge of the TSA agent and tried to make conversation.

"My father used to play the banjo," said Bruce's manager. "He often played a song called 'Sourwood Mountain.' Is that where you got your name? You'll have to forgive my ignorance. This is my first trip to the states. For all I know, there might be plenty of people named Sourwood. Are there many people with the surname Sourwood? Am I starting to ramble?"

"Yes, to the rambling," said Thomas. "No, to

the Sourwood. I've never heard of the song. What the hell happened to him?"

"To be perfectly honest," began Bruce's manager.

"Have you read Crazy Rhythm, by Nicolas Irons?" said Bruce. "It has got to be one of the most remarkable books I have ever read. Do you realize what a national treasure you have in this man?"

"Mr. Prise has a fear of flying," said his agent, "that being said, unfortunately his flight encountered a bit of turbulence."

"If you haven't read this book, you need to go out and get a copy of it right now!" said Bruce.

"Was he on anything while he was on the flight?" asked the customs agent.

"He takes some anti-anxiety medication just to deal with the flight, and the occasional sleeping pill, but that is it," said Bruce's manager. "He is supposed to be doing Mr. Willet's late night talk show tonight."

"Really!" said Thomas. "Mr. Willet, the self-proclaimed king of late night?"

"Yes," said the manager. "He's supposed to be doing both an interview segment as well as performing with his band."

"That man is a comedy legend!" said Thomas. "You need to get to your hotel so that you can get him cleaned up!"

"Actually, I think I may need to ask Mr. Prise a question or two," said the customs agent.

"No, what you need to do is shut your pie hole," said Thomas. "You gentlemen are free to go."

"I'm going to report you to Mrs. Frakes," said the customs agent.

"Good luck on the program," said Thomas. "If you get a moment to tell Mr. Willet, I'm his biggest fan."

"We sure will," said Bruce's manager.

Chapter Five

Wherein Mr. Willet almost goes for a run.

Mr. Willet had never been a big fan of flashy opulence. He embraced what most of the major magazines said about him, that he exuded an old school Hollywood charm. Most people could see him relaxing poolside with top shelf bourbon, and not making a big deal about it. He wouldn't be someone who would later have too much to drink and be sloppy. He wasn't one to trash a hotel room, or rape an intern.

There were only two things that Mr. Willet had an unhealthy obsession with: his comedy, and his fanatical adherence to proper grammar.

His grandmother had raised Mr. Willet. She had served in the first women's battalion in the United States Marine Corp. After that she brought her fierce sense of discipline to teaching. Most people agreed that they had never seen a more efficient or quieter first grade classroom in their life. She was also under the misconception that her daughter's fall from grace had been the result of a lack of discipline and proper grammar, instead of her crippling drug addiction. These lessons were ruthlessly beaten into Mr. Willet. His only respite was making his grandmother laugh.

"I don't know if I have it fucking in me, Ty," said Mr. Willet, as he sped along the 101 talking on his cell phone. "Maybe I should think about just saying goodbye to it all. They're talking about a three-year extension to my contract and to be perfectly honest I'm not sure if I have another three years in me."

"You sound awfully whiney right now," said Ty. "Have you been talking to your ex? You always get full of self-doubt whenever you talk to her. Why do you talk to her? As your manager haven't I told you to stop talking to her?"

"No, it isn't that," said Mr. Willet, as he narrowly avoided a collision with a semi, weaving in and out of lanes as only someone who was deeply familiar with Los Angeles traffic could. "I'm just not feeling it this season. I'm beginning to feel like we're starting to repeat ourselves. Unless we think about doing something fucking drastic, we're going to go down the tubes. Flushed away and forgotten like Ernie Fucking Kovacs!"

"Who?" said Ty.

"You disappoint me, Ty," said Mr. Willet. "I like you because you were one of the old timers."

"Stop whining like a little bitch," said Ty. "Go to the gym, then get your ass back to the studio. They want you in a writers meeting. They're preparing for the shows from Tokyo next week. There's something you've never done! You want to be fucking brilliant and groundbreaking? Then go be brilliant and break ground. Enough of this bullshit!"

Ty hung up and Mr. Willet's phone beeped at him, just to let him know that he was no longer actually speaking to anyone. Alone with his thoughts and the traffic, he sped up to the front of the West Encino Athletic Club.

The front of the exclusive gym, which had been designed by a world-renowned Spanish architect, wasn't marred with gaudy signage. There was simply the valet out front. The valet was discreet, shockingly well paid, and had memorized the cars of all of the members.

"Hello, Mr. Willet," said the valet, as he opened the car door for him. "Wonderful to see you today."

"And wonderful to see you as well, sir," said Mr. Willet. Mr. Willet had always had difficulty remembering people's names. However, he had a remarkable capacity to remember people's faces. To deflect his embarrassment for not knowing the valet's name, he overcompensated, treating most people with an obsequious amount of gentile respect, doting on them with a "sir" or "ma'am". Most people found it endearing.

"You must forgive my prying, Mr. Willet, but are you planning on a longer workout today?" said the valet. "I shouldn't pry, but they are working on the parking garage today, and if you are planning on a quick one today, I want to make you car very accessible."

"That is very thoughtful of you, sir," said Mr. Willet. "Unfortunately, it will be a quick one today."

"I'll keep it close then," said the valet.

As Mr. Willet watched his car pull off he made a mental note to visit the ATM in the gym, to ensure a good tip for the valet. The automatic doors, sensing the key fob buried deep in Mr.

Willet's custom leather gym bag, opened to reveal a four story, state of the art, climate controlled masterpiece. Simply calling the West Encino Athletic club a gym was insulting.

The open atrium in the center of the facility had fountains and sculptured bushes that would put some four star hotels to shame with their elegance and exquisite attention to detail. In the midst of the lobby was a large four story rock-climbing wall. Along the outside of the towering structure were balconies that showed small a glimpse into the weight rooms, yoga, and personalized non-denominational wellness studios. Within individual rooms were personalized climate controlled running simulators, which could recreate any terrain imaginable: from running the Great Wall of China, to a light jog through Central Park.

Mr. Willet had a standing reservation for his favorite run on weekdays when taping his late night program. It helped him clear his head. He thought helped him think outside the comedy box.

"Mr. Willet," said the trainer behind the desk, "how are you today?"

"Very well, ma'am," said Mr. Willet, smiling

warmly. "I'm here for my run."

"Yes," said the trainer. "Unfortunately, your usual room is having a few difficulties. So, today we've put you in one of the running simulators on the second floor. We are very sorry for any inconvenience this might cause. We have disinfected the room, and have your usual program loaded up."

Mr. Willet fought every urge he had to scream at the young woman. He knew rationally that it didn't matter. He was still going to get his run in, and once the simulator began there really was no way to tell in which room you were in. But, Mr. Willet thought that his art was tied directly to his routine. By sticking to a steady routine of magnificent repetition, it allowed his brain to become bored enough to wander, causing him to try to cure his boredom by daydreaming. The young female trainer didn't understand any of this; she just knew how many of the members would react to not being able to get want they wanted.

"Of course," said Mr. Willet. "Thank you for trying to make it right."

"That is want we're here for," said the trainer. "If you would be so kind as to follow me, I'll show you to your room."

Mr. Willet reluctantly followed the woman down the long corridor and up a flight of immaculate stairs, and down a second hallway. None of the doors were numbered.

"Here we are, Mr. Willet," she said.

Mr. Willet stared at the white door. In the center of it was a picture of a woman who was exerting herself. It was clear that the picture was supposed to be motivational. The woman was attractive, her naked torso appealing, and she filled a sports bra well. If he had been going to his regular room, he might not have even given it another thought, but there across the middle of the woman's sweaty torso, in bright orange Comic Sans font read, "Test you're metal."

"Is there something wrong, Mr. Willet?" asked the trainer.

"Why is that on the door?" said Mr. Willet. "And do you have any clue as to how wrong it is?"

"I knew you were clever Mr. Willet," said the trainer. "Yeah, the use of you are instead of the possessive your. You would be surprised how many people miss that. However, the woman who typically uses this room is the one in the ad. We keep it up to help her stay motivated."

"And hopefully assist her with her grammar," said Mr. Willet. "You do realize that it's the wrong kind of metal."

"I'm sorry?"

"It should read 'test your mettle' m-e-t-t-l-e."

"Look at you, I had no idea you were an armchair grammarian," said the trainer. "At risk of sounding contrary, I believe that they may be interchangeable. I mean, there are a myriad of rules and spellings that have changed over the centuries."

"No."

"Excuse me?" said the trainer.

"You don't say, 'myriad of'," said Mr. Willet. "The 'of' is already included."

"Okay," said the trainer, "ready for your run?"

"Don't be dismissive," said Mr. Willet, as his frustration, fear, and self-doubt, bubbled to the surface. "It is the English fucking language!"

"There is no reason to belittle me, Mr. Willet," said the trainer.

"I'm sorry I don't mean to belittle you, Miss" said Mr. Willet. "But, there is no way that I could possibly use this room, even if you removed the poster."

"I have no intention of removing the poster, Mr. Willet."

"Then, Miss, I believe we may have a problem."

"Why do you keep calling me, Miss?" said the Trainer. "You've never even bothered to learn my name, have you? I've only been greeting you at the front desk for the past four years. I might be able to understand if I hadn't been wearing a name tag, and you have the balls to be this much of an asshole to me?"

"Ummmm," said Mr. Willet, as he turned and ran back down the hallway. He was certain that there were myriad ways he could have extracted himself from that situation more elegantly. But, standing in the hallway he had never noticed how narrow it was, nor how oppressive the doors looked. Why would anyone paint doors that white? After a few hours they would never look that white again, would they?

Mr. Willet ran out of the gym.

The valet had his car waiting for him.

"I'm sorry I don't have anything for a tip,"

screamed Mr. Willet as he snatched the keys from the hand of the waiting valet.

"Don't you worry about it," said the valet, as the car sped off toward the freeway.

At rehearsal, Mr. Willet was distant, and maybe a bit more on edge than usual. There had been more than one occasion where he was reminded to make certain that the Aussie be ushered quickly over to lip sync to another song from his album. Had something to do with him and a bad flight. Mr. Willet wasn't listening. He was trying to listen. He knew he was supposed to be listening. The poster and the way the young woman had reacted played over and over again in his head.

This was why, when prompted to ask Bruce to play another song, he absentmindedly asked if he had read any good books.

Chapter Six

Wherein Nicolas suffers from writer's block.

     To say that the apartment was drafty was a lie. Nicolas could think of quite a few months where there was hardly a breeze in the cramped two-bedroom apartment. Sadly, this was most often the months of July, August and September. Once October hit, the windows in the ancient building would wait to see if there was going to be an Indian summer. Nicolas was amazed that the windows seemed to have their own internal thermostat. As soon as the temperature outside would begin to flirt with the thirties, they would allow a cross breeze that would come in off Lake Michigan, cross Lincoln Park, funnel up Lincoln Avenue, and through Nicolas' small two bedroom Lincoln Square apartment with the force of a mild gale, often blowing with enough ferocity to extinguish candles. Nicolas had become used to sharing his apartment with the brutal Chicago winters. He had fingerless gloves, and a few space heaters surrounding his desk in an arch while he wrote at his computer. He imagined he looked very reminiscent of Bob Cratchet, waiting for Mr. Scrooge to allow him to place another coal on the fire, with the exception that Nicolas was a good deal fatter that Mr. Cratchet.

Nicolas had talked to the landlord about the windows, however he saw how hard Mr. Paqin worked trying to keep the building together, he felt bad about putting too much pressure on him. Mr. Paqin had always been very patient with Nicolas, especially during months when he would need some extra time with the rent. Eventually, Nicolas reached his limit, and was ready to threaten to move unless something were done about the heat, but on that very day he discovered that he was published. A small science fiction and fantasy magazine had purchased three of his short stories. After that, Nicolas was of the mistaken impression that he needed to stay and continue to write in the small, drafty apartment. Much like an addict he thought pain was integral to his creative process.

His latest novella Crazy Rhythm had been

enjoying steady success, not enough that he was a household name, but enough that he took a chance and quit his day job to focus on his writing full time. There are some people who when they remove the white noise of daily life they can finally devote everything they have to their process. In the new peaceful serenity left alone with their thoughts they can mine the depths of their creativity for wonderful prose. Others, when left alone with themselves, freak out. Nicolas freaked out. Nicolas thrived on escaping from the absurdity of the daily struggle that was living and working in a city like Chicago. But, left with nothing to escape from, he developed writers block.

Nicolas hoped that his usual touchstones would assist in breaking him out of his funk. A visit to the Art Institute left him feeling inadequate. Drinking heavily made him feeble the next morning. A road trip out of the city resulted in a six car pile up, a block from the interstate.

He sat in front of his computer staring at the blank screen, trying to will an idea into existence. He tried free association, writing prompts, even free verse poetry. He tried freeing himself from distractions, by disconnecting his computer from the internet, and placing his cell phone in the bottom of his sock drawer.

After ten days he had only written the word "fuck" four-thousand six-hundred and forty-two times, and the phrase "mother fucker" sixteen times, and "poop" twice. Out of toilet paper and wine, he ventured out for the first time in nearly a week. The air was crisp, a light snow falling. It was an ideal winter day, but Nicolas saw none of it. What he did see was the large group of women doing yoga on the ground floor of the new gym in the neighborhood. The idea, Nicolas thought, was an inspired one. Go and do something physical, the Zen act of repetition, might just allow him to generate an idea!

"Hello," said the woman at the front desk, who had shockingly white teeth.

"Yes," said Nicolas I think I might want to join your athletic club," said Nicolas.

"Allow me to get one of our membership advisors," said the woman.

"Do you really have to?" said Nicolas. "I was just hoping I could join."

"Don't you want to take a tour of the facility

first?"

"Not really, I would just rather join if I could," said Nicolas.

"I don't think that is allowed. I think you have to take the tour, have a brief orientation, a physical assessment by our personal training staff, and then you have to sign the membership agreement."

"Oh," said Nicolas. "I'm just here to try to make a change."

"Most people do," said the woman. "Don't worry. The membership advisor will be out momentarily."

"Thank you?"

"You're very welcome."

With how nice everyone was being to Nicolas, he was beginning to doubt the wisdom behind walking into the athletic club in the first place. It looked nice enough. The ground floor was dominated by the reception desk and a large staircase. One side led up to the actual gym, and the other down to the locker area. The large skylight above the stairs made the place look annoyingly bright. None of the people he saw looked as if they were in intimidating shape. They looked like normal people, but then again, most cults do look relatively normal from the outside, thought Nicolas.

"Hi, I'm Mindy," said the very tan woman, who was trying to shake his hand. Her teeth were even whiter than the receptionist's. She was dressed professionally in clothes that were just tight enough to be distracting.

"Hi, Mindy," said Nicolas. "I'm Nicolas."

"Cool, so you're interested in joining the club?" said Mindy.

"I think," said Nicolas.

"Well, let's take the tour," said Mindy as she led him up the stairs.

One side of the large open space was full of cardio equipment, each having its own private television screen. The other side was a large free weight room, with a beautiful dance floor for stretching in the center. Mindy didn't say much; she knew the space was impressive, she didn't need to sell it.

"So, Nicolas what do you do?" said Mindy.

Nicolas didn't hear her ask the question. He was fixated on what was on the television screen attached to one of the stair climbers. There on the television, was his book. For some reason they were talking about his book on whatever channel the television was set to.

"Um, sir," said Mindy. "If you'd like to continue."

"What are they saying," said Nicolas. "Sorry, I'm an idiot, why would you know what they're talking about?"

Mindy took a quick look at the silent television screen, "Oh, they're talking about <u>Crazy Rhythm</u> have you read it? Horrible title, amazing book."

"How did you hear about it?"

"Are you insane? For the past week it is all anyone can talk about, after that Australian guy talked about it on Mr. Willet's late night program. Everyone's been trying to get in touch with the guy who wrote it, some kind of a recluse. Local too!"

Nicolas pulled his cell phone out of his pocket; to his surprise, he had forty-seven voice mails.

"I'm sorry, sir," said Mindy. "We try to restrict member's cell phone use to the lobby."

"Ummmm," said Nicolas, as he ran toward the stairs, "that's okay."

His phone began to vibrate once he reached the lobby.

"Hello?" he said, after hitting the large green answer button. He had to hit it multiple times. His hands were shaking and for some strange reason covered in sweat.

"Nicolas, why the fuck haven't you been answering your phone?" Nicolas recognized the voice as an old friend from college who was now living out in Los Angeles. She did something in the world of film, although he couldn't remember what.

"I had writer's block, Christina," said Nicolas.

"Well, then you just go back to having writer's block and don't answer another call," said Christina. "Make sure you delete all your messages. Don't even bother to listen to them. I'm catching a flight to Chicago. I should be there tomorrow afternoon."

"Do you have me on speaker phone?" said Nicolas.

"Yes," said Christina. "I'm driving. Is that a problem?"

"Is there anyone in the car with you?"

"Yes, my assistant."

"Fuck, why didn't you tell me there was

someone in the car with you?"

"What does it fucking matter?" said Christina. "You haven't been answering your goddamned phone for the past week. Why am I going to waste my time finding a quiet corner to talk to you if I don't even know if you are going to pick up the fucking phone?"

"I just feel like an asshole."

"Then stop acting like one. Listen, you remember that crappy German bar you used to live across the street from? The one we got shit-faced in a while back."

"Yes, I still live across from it."

"Really?"

"Yeah."

"Well, that's about to change. Meet me there tomorrow evening, six-ish. And what ever you do, don't answer your fucking phone, or look through your e-mail. Everything is about to explode for you in an amazing fucking way!"

Nicolas delicately slid the phone back into his pocket.

"So," said Mindy. "Would you like to check out the locker rooms?"

Chapter Seven

Wherein Mr. Willet doesn't rape anyone.

Mr. Willet pretended that the conversations he had been having over the past few days had been productive; that maybe he hadn't been obsessing over the small piece of paper on the door of the private running simulator at the West Encino Athletic club; that he hadn't passed three billboards in the past week with the same image and offensive grammatical errors on them. He had watched news reports extolling the slight charm of the signs, completely ignoring the use of the incorrect "metal". Mr. Willet wiped away tears of frustration.

He tried to bring up these issues to people, but they just thought he was charming. Both his tenacity in exposing grammatical inaccuracies as well as his vehement denouncement of those who butcher the English language. But, they never noticed the "metal". Or, if they did they would say something glib, regarding the colloquial usage of the phrase, making its glaring inaccuracies acceptable, or at the very least, slightly less deplorable.

He sat quietly through the production meeting, nodding when he assumed he should. He smiled through the majority of the writers' meeting, finalizing the opening monologue as well as the sketches. He almost seemed to fall asleep during his makeup and wardrobe call. Most of the production staff was surprised at how centered and relaxed Mr. Willet appeared. However, just under the surface he was primed to crack; the voices screaming out in his head to correct the grammatical injustice that was before him. But, as Mr. Willet began his pre-show warm up, all of it melted away. He was and had always prided himself on being a professional.

After the warm up he began his pre-show rituals. They were small touchstones, which helped him continue to focus. Many of them were superstitious like knocking three times on the stage door before heading behind the curtain to wait for his entrance. He smiled at the stage manager and they shared the same secret handshake they had before every show. Then as the band began to play, he would look toward the rafters to give one of the grips a nod and a smile. The curtain would part and Mr. Willet walked out to the adulation of the studio audience.

Mr. Willet had never been a fan of cue cards, preferring to memorize most of what was going on during the program, especially his monologue, and sketches. Therefore it was no surprise to him when the latest news model of the moment came out from behind the curtain in the middle of his monologue. She was there to quickly promote her move from local news to a national sports news channel. Both stations were owned by the same parent company that also owned the network that Mr. Willet's program was on. Mr. Willet hadn't much liked the idea, but he had worked out a quick skit with the young woman, and once he began rehearsing with her, he found her charming and pleasantly disarming.

Once Mr. Willet had reached the point where he was supposed to turn and realize she was behind him, he did so with the relaxed nonchalance of a true professional, until he registered what she was wearing. Across her chest were the words, "Test

You're Metal." The shirt itself was a full size too small; making her already generous endowments look even larger. The crowd went wild when they saw her. At fist she assumed that Mr. Willet's pause was due to how the shirt flattered her figure.

The crowd began to giggle, as Mr. Willet stood there speechless.

"This is the moment," said Tyler, Mr. Willet's Manager, as he pressed pause on the tape, the speechless image of Mr. Willet frozen on the screen. "From here you could have just walked away, continued with the skit, feigned a heart attack. There are so many fucking things you could have done that would have been alright."

"Ty, do we really need to watch this?" said Mr. Willet, as he stared out the small window in Tyler's office onto the Hollywood Hills. A plume of black smoke rose from far behind the Hollywood sign.

"Fuck, you think I want to fucking watch this again?" said Tyler. "You think I want to watch you barrage the poor girl, and then rip her shirt off while she cries. Jesus Fucking Christ, you almost looked like you were raping her! You weren't actually trying to rape her were you?"

"Of course I wasn't," said Mr. Willet. "I guess it was just a momentary lapse in judgment." The black smoke in the distance changed to white.

"No, you fucking lunatic," said Tyler. "Getting drunk and cracking up your car, is a momentary lapse in judgment. Getting caught with a trio of hookers in Vegas is a momentary lapse in judgment. This is a fucking shit-storm!"

"Maybe it's time," said Mr. Willet. "Maybe I need to just walk away. The ideas just aren't coming the way they used to."

"You're lucky. You realize that don't you? At some point someone reached down and kissed you on the ass to say that you were going to be spared."

"What are you talking about?"

"The poor girl you nearly raped will not press charges. I talked her out of it. She's one of my other clients, as is the woman in that dumb ass ad you've decided to have a goddamned vendetta over! Why do you feel the need to deprive either of these poor girls the success they deserve? They aren't the morons who wrote that stupid copy in the first place. You want to get pissed at someone go over to the advertising agency on Wilshire and scream at the fucking asshat who wrote copy for that ad. Or, even better, get pissed at me. I'm the one who kept the story alive for my client. I thought it was funny. So, tell me, do you want to fucking yell at me? Do you want to rape me?"

"Of course not, Ty," said Mr. Willet, as he continued to look out at the smoke.

"Here is what is going to happen," said Tyler. "First, you're going to go and relax for a bit, take that trip to Japan you've been talking about for so long. Then, when you get back and all of this has blown over, we can see about you issuing some sort of apology. Then we get you back on the air."

"Wait, what do you mean back?" said Mr. Willet.

"Since no one is pressing charges," said Tyler, "the network has agreed to allow you back after you take some time off to get your shit together."

"No!" said Mr. Willet. "No, I can't do this anymore. Why the hell didn't they fire me?"

"Calm down," said Tyler. "You can thank me later."

"I don't want to thank you," said Mr. Willet. "I thought I was done."

"Look," said Tyler, "you're not thinking right.

You've got your head up your ass. Go take some time, relax. Get your ass to Japan. And I promise you, while you are there your entire perspective is going to change. You're going to be coming up with ideas that you're not going to be able to keep to yourself. You'll bring back such new comedy, such brilliant stuff, they'll be begging to give you another fucking Emmy!"

Mr. Willet walked quietly out of the office. He had always loved the old building that housed Tyler's office. In strict defiance of the neighborhood's constant gentrification, it still retained a good deal of its 20's Hollywood charm. Mr. Willet bounded down the grand staircase and out onto Sunset Boulevard. He fought the urge to run. All he wanted to do was start running and not stop until things made sense. Instead he drove home for his passport, packed a small duffle bag, purchased a first class ticket to Tokyo, and left.

Chapter Eight

Wherein Nicolas explores the scourge of
gentrification.

Nicolas stood out in front of the bar. He used
to enjoy going to bars, until hipsters had invaded
the neighborhood. He knew every successive wave
of gentrification feels the same contempt for the
wave that follows them, especially if they view
themselves as some kind of trailblazers. Nicolas
used to enjoy hanging out with the townies. The old
guard was half the fun of the place. They would
awkwardly stare at you until they realized that you
weren't there to judge them, or they just got too
drunk to care. Nicolas never insisted on artisanal
bitters or contrived cocktails. He hoped that he
wasn't quite as reviled as the sea of skinny jeans
that had claimed the bar for their own.

Christina sat in the middle of it all with her
own relaxed confidence that only people who came

from California seemed to exude. Nicolas wasn't surprised by how tan she was, but was shocked at how pale everyone else seemed in comparison. She spotted Nicolas and waved in a goofy manner that only someone who was truly confident in who they were could pull off. Nicolas sighed and walked into the bar.

Inside it was warm and humid. A song he didn't recognize was playing on the new "songmaster" in the corner. He thought about walking over to see what the name of it was, but it wouldn't matter. He wouldn't recognize the name of the obscure band anyway. If he did they never would have played it.

"Nick!" said Christina, as she waved him over to her table. "It is fantastic to see you!"

"Hi, Christina," said Nicolas.

"What is with this formality?" she said. "Relax. You know better, call me Chris."

"Sure if you call me Nicolas."

"Really," said Christina, "I haven't see you in years, and you're going to kick off this reunion by being an asshole?"

"I'm not being an asshole."

"Yes, Nicolas you are being an asshole," said

Christina. "I'm here in town to talk to you about making a ridiculous amount of money."

"That you're going to want ten percent of."

"See," said Christina, "this is what I'm talking about."

"Fine, should we start over?" said Nicolas. "How's Jack?"

"We got divorced six months ago," said Christina, as she signaled to the bartender that they needed another round. "Are you fine with a cocktail?"

"What is in it?"

"Damned if I know," said Christina. "But it tastes amaze balls."

"Don't say that."

"Say what?"

"Amaze balls," said Nicolas. "It is almost as insipid as awesomsauce."

"Insipid?" said Christina. "You're actually going to sit across the table from me and use the word insipid with a straight face? Tell me, have you been waiting all day to whip out your word of the day, or do bullshit elitist phrases just roll off the tongue for you now?"

"I'm sorry," said Nicolas. "I'm sorry you got

a divorce as well."

"Why?" she said. "It is a hell of a lot better than still being married to that asshat."

"I liked, Jack," he said.

"Honey, nobody liked, Jack. Jack was an asshole."

"Can I have the juicer back?" said Nicolas.

"What juicer?"

"The one I got you for your wedding present," said Nicolas. "It took me the better part of an entire day, six different El's and a cab to find the right one."

"Oh, yeah," said Christina. "Right before we got married he was deep into this juice cleanse. That was why we put it on our registry."

"So, can I have it back?" said Nicolas.

"First, that is kind of rude," said Christina. "Why would you ask someone if they could have a present back? Second it doesn't matter. He sold it online."

"Why?"

"Because, they wouldn't let him return it after he used it for a month. Told you he was an asshole."

The bartender brought over a pair of

cocktails. Christina looked at her and gave her a warm smile and fifty dollar bill.

"I have no clue what you put in this, but it is remarkable," said Christina. "If you notice us getting about half way through these we would love another round."

"How do you know I want another round if I haven't even tried it?" said Nicolas.

"Please ignore him, he's being an asshole," said Christina. The bartender smiled and returned to the other customers at the bar.

"Why did you have to do that?" said Nicolas.

"If you'd stop whining for five minutes, I might just be able to get to what I wanted to talk to you about."

"Which is?"

"I want you to come out to Los Angeles next week and take a few meetings."

"Meetings?"

"Yes, it's what civilized people do before they write you big checks to make movies from shit you write."

"Why would anyone want to make a movie out of one of my books?"

"I don't claim to understand what is going to

be hot and what isn't, if I did I would have been here long before some Aussie went batshit over your book," said Christina. "That was all it took to put you on the best seller list. Right now your book is so goddamn hot that we could film a fucking monkey in a diaper for a hundred and twenty minutes and as long as it said it was based on your book we'd walk away with a shit-ton of money."

"So let's find a monkey."

"Fuck you," said Christina. "Let's option the rights for more money than we should, and then let some other asshole deal with the filming, editing, and marketing."

"I don't know."

"Look, if you're in the middle of your next masterpiece, then we can bring your laptop. Relax in L.A. for a couple of days. We'll fly you out, put you up in a nice hotel. You smile and pretend you're not an asshole for five minutes, get a tan and come home with a fuck-load more money than when you left."

"I'll have to think about it."

"What is there to think about? Don't think. Drink your cocktail, say yes, and then we can have another."

"I'm sorry. I just have a lot going on right now."

"Writer's block?"

"Maybe," said Nicolas.

"I thought so," said Christina. "I know you, and when you get like this it's because you're hoping your routine will help you. Trust me. There's no more routine. You're on three different fucking bestseller lists. Did you do the whole indie thing with this book as well?"

"Yeah, how did you know?"

"It doesn't matter," said Christina. "You make what two, maybe three bucks a book? So, by virtue of some Aussie gushing over your book, you're a fucking millionaire. You didn't even think about that did you?"

"Fuck."

"Yeah, I didn't think you had. Everyone wants to option this book."

"Have they read it?"

"Probably not, but that isn't going to stop a bidding war for the rights," said Christina. "But, that is only going to happen if we get you out there to start taking meetings next week."

"I don't know," said Nicolas.

"What the hell is there to know?" said Christina. "Either you come out and we get a big ass deal together, or you come out and you get a tan, a quick change of perspective and then you're back here, hopefully, not still suffering from writer's block."

"Fine," said Nicolas, as he drained his cocktail. "Holy shit what was that?"

"Fuck if I know," she said. "I'll send someone by with the tickets."

Nicolas ran out of the bar and onto the cold street, no longer able to resist the urge to vomit, and heaved into a waste bin.

A couple pushing a small child in a stroller crossed to the other side of the street to avoid Nicolas.

Christina waved to him from inside the warm bar.

Chapter Nine

The second excerpt from Crazy Rhythm by Nicolas
Irons

Anton looked up through the snow. The
heavy flakes hit him hard in the face. If he weren't
so cold already it might have stung. The
paratrooper hung there in the tree. He swung back
and forth in the wind. Anton looked across the
empty field. This was the only tree for over five
acres. Anton had never jumped out of a plane
before. Anton had never been on a plane before.
Still he assumed that it must have been some very
poor luck to get caught in the only tree in the
otherwise wide-open field. Anton knew about bad
luck. His grandmother had always told him that
his bad luck was due to being saddled with a
Russian name, rather than a solid Belgian one.

Until now, Anton had been willing to agree
with his grandmother. But, looking up at the warm

clothes on the dead paratrooper, he felt that his luck might be changing. He looked down at his blue feet and walked across the frozen mud to the tree. Pulling himself up to the lowest branch was slow going. He felt like his thin arms were burning with exhaustion, but it felt different from the cold. Anything different from the cold was a good thing.

A solid gust threatened to knock him out of the tree. Anton turned to the wind and screamed. He knew that it would do no good, but it made him feel better. Clutching tighter to the branches, he slowly climbed up to the branch the body was hanging from. Looking at the ropes that were tangled in the thick branches, he laughed. He knew that unless he used his teeth, there was going to be no way he could get the body down. He was going to have to be a little rat, gnawing through the ropes. He let out the sound of a little squeak, and began laughing again.

He placed his head low to the branch and tried to bite the rope. As he did a strong, cold wind gust caused him to loose his footing. Falling, he reached out wildly, trying to grab anything to help him stop his fall, anything so he wouldn't have to climb back up and try again. He grabbed something, big and thick, but it gave way, and Anton slammed hard on the frozen mud. The wind knocked out of him, he gasped for air, and tried to push the heavy load he had ripped down from the tree with him. It was difficult to shift, but as he slowly began breathing again, he calmly moved the load, and rolled it off him.

Anton wobbled to his feet and looked up. The body was gone. Anton looked at the tree and laughed. This must have been a hallucination. Here he was in the middle of this field, and soon he would freeze to death. He might as well giggle his way into oblivion. Then he tripped over the body.

The uniform fit well, a bit baggy, but not bad. The first issue Anton had with the outfit was the shoes. They were two sizes too big. Anton didn't mind, even shoes that would give him blisters would be better than no shoes at all. The second issue was the belt. It was so heavy, full of guns and ammunition. How anyone thought a belt with so much on it would keep a pair of pants up was ridiculous. The final issue was the pack. Anton thought it must be full of more ammunition. He couldn't imagine what else could make it so heavy.

Then he opened it to see bars of chocolate and cigarettes.

Anton squealed, and tore into the first bar of chocolate he touched. After eating half of it, he had stopped shaking and began to unload the heavy pack to see what else was in it. He removed the ammunition, explosives, and papers, and placed them with the body. The cans of soup, meat and cigarettes he left in the pack. The chocolate bars he loaded into the ammunition packs on his belt.

With the pack much lighter, a cigarette in his mouth, and chocolate in his belly, the distance to the other side of the field wasn't as daunting.

Covering the ground quickly, he soon found shelter in the tree line on the other side. On this side the forrest was not as thick, he would have to be careful.

But, thought Anton, it is much easier to be careful with chocolate in your belly. It makes one much less desperate.

"Well, I have to say that it is very good to see you making the most of this," said Uncle Hans's voice.

"As am I, Uncle," said Anton. "Would you care for a cigarette?"

"No, thank you," said Uncle Han's voice. "I think I'm thin enough already."

"I wouldn't say that," said Anton, as he turned to see him sitting at the kitchen table.

"Do you want to tell us what happened?" said Anton's wife. He was happy to see her again. He grabbed her and kissed her deeply. She pulled away, blushing slightly, her hand trying to hide her broad smile.

"Anton, I was in the middle of asking Uncle a question," she said.

"That is true, you were, but I think in that moment it was much more important for Anton to kiss you," said Uncle Hans. "And so he should. This is all much too serious. We should go out tonight! I have some friends I need to talk to at the theaters, and then we shall go out for a feast!"

A small cough came from the other room.

"I'm not sure that would be a good idea," said Anton's wife. "It is a very different place since you've last been Uncle."

"I know," said Uncle Hans. "Sadly, that is the way it is everywhere, but here there is hope. That is why I came. I am going to make certain that this hope is something that is shared with your whole family! So no more long faces! I will have Anton escort me to see a few friends, then we will return with a large loaf of bread, and a nice bottle of wine, and have ourselves a feast here!"

"At the risk of sounding rude, I will believe it when I see it," said Anton's wife. "I haven't seen an ounce of flour in the city for months, let alone a bottle of wine."

"Then it is high time we get you some of both, my beautiful lady," said Uncle Hans. "Anton, while you get me my hat I need you to tell me how you got a woman as wonderful as you to marry a schmuck like you."

"Luck," said Anton.

"Got that right," said Anton's wife.

"Then you will be the perfect escort for me tonight," said Uncle Hans. "We will need as much luck as we can muster."

Hans and Anton exited the building to find the fog had become more oppressive and colder. The fine mist bit into Anton's skin.

"Anton," said Uncle Hans. "You had better hide."

"What?" said Anton.

"There is a convoy coming," said Hans. "You need to lay down in the snow right now."

Anton looked down at the oversized boots on his feet. He was no longer standing on the small cobblestone street outside his building. He was in the trees. Through them he could see a small road, and hear the trucks.

Anton dove to the ground. He waited to hear the trucks pass. He allowed an eye to check to see how many trucks there were. Six total, and they all seemed more interested in putting distance between themselves and whatever was further down the road, that they didn't even bother to take a look at the field.

The motors of the trucks faded slowly into the muffled distance. Anton rose, and brushed the snow off himself. He made for the road, with the full knowledge that he needed to stay unseen in the wood, but wanted to see what had scared off the convoy. Or, maybe see if it led to a village or town of some kind?

"I think that is a very sound idea," said Uncle Hans' voice.

"Thank you," said Anton. "I thought so as

well."

"Shall we then?" said Uncle Hans, who was pointing the way up the small cobblestone street.

"No," said Anton. "We shouldn't go that way."

"But, that's the way to the theatre district," said Uncle Hans. "Or have I gotten myself completely turned around?"

The streetlights began to flicker on.

"No, you're right, but we have to go this way," said Anton.

Uncle Hans moved to protest, and then simply stated, "Discretion is the better part of valor. Please, Anton, lead the way."

"I understand your issue," said Hans from behind the door. "I don't want to make things more difficult for you. I truly don't. But, there must be something. I'll even work flying in the sets."

"I have sandbags that weight more than you," said the theatre owner.

This had been the way it had been at the previous four theaters as well. Anton knew better than anyone how sparse jobs were, but this was Uncle Hans. Anton wasn't trying to listen but the door was thin and he was just beginning to get a little less hopeful for the bottle of wine and the loaf of bread promised to his wife.

He peered slightly around the curtain to see what was going on onstage. A group of very attractive girls were singing a beautiful tune. One was playing a banjo while the other was playing a violin. The band in the orchestra was keeping up with them, but only just. It was a quick jazz tune that Anton couldn't place, but he liked it. He had always liked the sound of the banjo. He thought it sounded happy.

"You must understand what a draw I am," said Hans.

"Back in Germany, ten years ago I bet you would bring down the house," said the theatre owner. "But, here, I just don't have-"

"There must be something," said Hans. "Please."

The theatre owner sighed deeply. "I'm going to regret this. I know I am going to regret this, but tell me can you   work a marionette?"

"I got my start on the street working a marionette show for children."

"Great you'll be doing that again," said the theatre owner. "You'll be working the matinees."

"Will you let me do a night show?" begged Uncle Hans.

"If we have an opening to fill, we'll see. Just be here tomorrow for the matinee for the kids."

"Thank you," said Hans.

The door opened and Hans emerged from the theatre office with a wide grin on his face.

"Things, are looking up, Anton," said Hans. "See, all you have to do is be willing to put in as little bit of elbow grease and the world doesn't seem all that unmanageable does it?"

The girls came running off stage.

"Now" said Hans, "all we need to do is find ourselves a bottle of wine."

"Are you sure, Uncle Hans?" said Anton. "Maybe we should just think about calling it a day."

"Nonsense," said Hans. "You should never underestimate the ingenuity of a desperate actor, especially one who likes to drink! Why don't you start by looking over there?"

Anton turned see where he was pointing.

A small hut was standing in the middle of the wood. Of course, standing is a very relative term. It leaned to one side, impeded in its slow progress toward earth by a large tree. Anton walked toward the hut. He had seen a few of these from the road. He had tried to steer clear of them. He didn't know what they were, but assumed that they housed soldiers waiting. That was the way it was. There was a soldier behind every corner waiting to kill you. This had to be some kind of a checkpoint. Anton came around the side of the hut to reveal that it wasn't a hut, but actually an outhouse.

"I don't think we're going to find very much for us in there, Uncle," said Anton as he giggled.

"Why not, you never quite know what you're going to find until you actually open the door do you?"

"I don't think I want to," said Anton.

"Anton," said Hans, who was standing next to him on the street. "All you have to do is pop in and pop out. I'm not asking you to take anything specific, just grab the first two you can find."

"It just doesn't seem right," said Anton. The large oak door in front of him had heavy black iron hinges, and a large lock. How Hans had gotten the door open was beyond him.

"Don't worry about that Anton," said Hans.

"There has been so much wrong going on lately, that bending the rules a little here and there is nothing compared to the atrocities going on around us. Take a deep breath. I absolve you. Go."

Hans pulled back the heavy oak door and Anton slipped in. The door closed revealing how dark the stairwell was. Anton slowly began his decent down the heavy stone stairs. This was the first time Anton had been in any of the houses in this part of the neighborhood. He would pass the guild houses with his wife and think about what they were like on the inside. He never understood how someone could fill that much space with their life. He had lived in apartments his whole life. The idea of not living in a building with other families seemed lonely.

Anton turned another corner; he could see a faint light at the end of the stairwell, through the arch at the next landing. Anton was unsure if this was a light that was always on, or maybe if someone was down there. If someone else had the same idea, and was now lying in wait at the bottom of the stairs. Anton walked down the remaining stairs very slowly.

At the bottom he peered through the arch,

there he saw an older man weeping openly over the body of a small child. The child had been placed on a large wood table in the middle of the room. Candles on the wall illuminated the scene. Anton's presence made them flicker slightly. The old man didn't notice. Anton thought about beating a quick retreat, but then saw his prize. Less than four feet from him, was the beginning of the wine cellar. Racks upon racks of wine just sitting in the stone basement. Anton stepped out of the archway quietly, pulled the two nearest bottles off the rack, and began walking back toward the stairs.

"It doesn't bother me that you're taking it," said the man. "It would have been nice to be asked, but that might be asking too much."

"I don't know," said Anton, fearful of turning around and having to face the old man over the body.

"Of course you don't, why would you?" said the man. "We aren't built for times like these. We used to be. Once we could deal with the savagery that went on around us, but not now. Now we've gotten soft, we've been conditioned to stop at red lights, only drive on certain sides of the street. To respect what is yours and what is mine, to not rape, to not murder, to not steal. Do you understand?"

"No," said Anton. "And I'm getting a little scared."

"Of course you are," said the man, his voice sounding closer. "You've been caught. Your body is pumping itself full of adrenaline, preparing its fight or flight instinct. Ready to tear off at a moment's notice, or stand your ground. Tell me my little thief, what will it be?"

Anton tore up the stairs. The old man's laughter chased him up the stairs. At the top of the stairs the door was stuck. Placing the bottles of wine on the stair behind him, he wedged his hands between the door and the jam, hoping that it would yield to his brute force. Finally, the door swung open.

Anton stood there looking at the dead body sitting in the outhouse. The snow began coming down harder. He looked at the body and wondered how he had died. The body tipped and fell forward onto the snow in front of Anton. The back of his skull was missing. It was a strange sight. The blood had drained from him, however with the cold weather the body had just frozen. There were no flies, no stench of rotting meat. The brains in the man's head looked more like something he would find at a deli than in a body. Anton hastily checked the pockets of the man, which were around his ankles. On the back of the door hung the man's coat. He could see the bright red armband.

Anton raised the borrowed boot and brought it down hard on the exposed brain. The skull gave way. Anton spit on the dead body, and then lifted his foot, but the boot would not come. He looked down to see what he had done. The boot itself was caught on a jagged piece of the soldier's skull. As Anton tried to lift his foot, the body came with the boot. Anton panicked, he kicked at the head hard with his other boot. The rest of the skull gave way, and Anton was free. He looked at the now liberated brain on the ground and spit.

"Thank you," said a tiny voice.

Anton looked around to see the source of the voice.

"Look," said Hans. "Just because you've never been a fan of calves brains, doesn't mean no one else will enjoy it."

Anton looked at the rest of the butcher's

case. "How's about a nice liver?" said Anton.

"Not tonight, not with the bottles of wine you've secured us!" said Hans. "I hope that you understand as well. Please tell me you do. I don't want to have to go through the tiresome dance that we're going to have to do. I'll be honest with you Mr. Butcher, as long as you promise to be straight with me. You do promise to be straight with me don't you?"

"Of course I will, sir," said the butcher.

"In that case show me the good stuff," said Hans.

"I'm certain I don't know what you mean," said the butcher.

"Of course you do, and I'll be honest with you," said Hans. "We are running a little bit late, aren't we Anton?"

"Not very," said Anton.

"Come now, we've kept your wife waiting long enough," said Hans. "Now, haven't I been more than honest with you,mand you are mocking my earnestness with your feints of ignorance. To be honest, I find it insulting."

Uncle Hans and the butcher stood there and glared at each other. They were sizing each other up. It appeared that neither Hans, nor the butcher were going to give an inch. Then finally the butcher blinked.

"I'm sorry," said the Butcher. "I have a beautiful pork loin."

"What do you take us for, those bastards?"

"You're right," said the butcher. "I've got a nice chicken."

"Much better," said Hans. "Wrap it up, well enough that we may be able to sneak it by everyone we need to."

The butcher disappeared into the back for a moment, and then returned with a nondescript box.

"Heavy," said Uncle Hans approvingly, as he handed the box to Anton. "Wait outside while I discus payment with this fine man."

Anton opened he door to the street and stepped out into the forest.

The wind bit at his face. Anton smiled back at the wind. It wasn't cutting through him like it had before. He could deal with cold cheeks. He pulled out another chocolate bar and began to eat as he trudged through the snow.

The clouds were beginning to thicken. Anton looked up at the grey sky as the clouds began to look darker and darker.

"You're going to have to start looking for a place to sleep," said his wife's voice.

"I'm not sure if that is the best of ideas," said Anton.

"You can't keep on like this," said his wife. "You're going to collapse. You need to sleep." She said trying to lead him over the threadbare rug to the bedroom.

"No," said Anton. "I need to see if I can find Uncle."

"He'll be fine," she said. "I don't want you to worry about him. You just go and get some sleep."

"I promise you, let me just go and check the theatre quickly," said Anton. "I'll be back before you know it."

"And if you're not?" she said.

A small cough came from the bedroom.

"Then you know what to do," he said.

"Hurry," she said.

Anton ran out into the street. There were screams. Things had been quiet. Things had been manageable, but it was changing. The occupation hadn't been easy, but it was one of those things that if you could understand the way that things worked, you would be alright, and Anton early on had understood the way things were supposed to work. But, now things were changing, and changing so rapidly that he couldn't keep up.

There were things on fire in the street. When did that ever happen? When did you turn a corner, and just see random things on fire? That didn't happen, not in this day and age. The soldiers were pulling people out of their apartments and dragging them into the street. This was why Anton needed to find Uncle Hans. He had not returned to the apartment for the past few days.

Since his arrival he had gone on the occasional bender, but nothing to this extreme. He would usually show up a night or two later, apologizing, and explaining that he had spent the night with a friend to give Anton and his family some space. Anton thought that the explanation was thoughtful of him, and made him look more courteous than he actually was, but the truth, that he was drunk and with a woman, would be worse. But, two nights before the latest spat of violence broke out, the provisional authority had closed the theaters.

Hans could not be found.

Anton stepped out of the building and onto a cold strange street. The small village had been nestled in a small valley. With one road through the town, it might have been spared, but it appeared that the soldiers had been very thorough. The contents of the small cottages that lined the only paved street in town had been emptied or burned. A few frozen bodies lay just inside doorways. Anton looked and saw the destruction that had been wrought on this poor town. He walked up the quiet street, along which the small cottages grew into shops. Anton tried the door to one of the shops. It opened.

Anton stepped through the stage door. The backstage which only a short while earlier had been a bustle with activity was now desolate. He could hear his Uncle's voice from the stage. Anton rushed toward the sound, and was met by a wild looking man, who was guarding access to the stage.

"Where do you think you're going!" said the

wild looking man.

"My Uncle, I think he's onstage right now," said Anton.

"Of course he is, and do you want to go and interrupt him?" said the wild man. "He's in the middle of his performance."

"Performance?"

"Why don't you head out into the house?" said the wild man. "Once he's done I'll send someone to escort you back to see him."

Anton looked at the crazed eyes of the old man, and walked down the small stairs and opened the door.

Anton emerged in the house of the theatre. The velvet seats had been slashed, burned, and defaced.

Uncle Hans was naked onstage with a pair of marionettes. Anton knew that Uncle had lost weight, but the way his skin hung off him made him look like a sick elephant.

"There is no escape!" said one of the puppets to the other.

"No, there is redemption!" screamed the other. "You will find it with our leader! All will find redemption with our leader."

Uncle brought out a third marionette. Anton thought it had been a poor attempt at a Charlie Chaplin, something for the kids, to look at the Little Tramp and giggle. But, now Uncle had modified the small man. He had removed the bowler, and the tattered clothes, replacing them with a crisp tan suit and a red armband. Uncle marched the little man across the stage. He was screaming in German as his face grew redder and redder.

"Uncle!" screamed Anton.

Hans stood there for a moment, and turned his eyes slowly toward Anton. A beautiful look of calm recognition came over Uncle's face.

"Anton?" said Uncle Hans. "Is that you? Did you get the wine?"

"Yes, Uncle," said Anton. "I have the wine. Get your things, and let's see our way home, shall we?"

"Right away," said Hans. "But, would it be alright if I brought my friend?"

"Who?" said Anton. "The man backstage."

"Nein!" said the marionette, as he goose-stepped over to Anton. "I shall go too, ya?"

"Uncle," said Anton. "We need to go, please."

"I don't think he'll let me go without him,"

said Hans.

"What if you left him with your friend backstage?" said Anton. I'm certain that he will take very good care of him."

"Nein!" Hans made the puppet say. "You think you can walk around this city without me? Do you have any idea who I am? And you want to leave me with that fool backstage?"

"Fine, you can come, but we have to leave now, and you have to be quiet!"

"How dare you tell me that I need to be quiet! Who do you think you are to tell me what I should do?"

"Uncle, please, we need to go," said Anton.

"Why?" said the voice behind them. "Are you afraid you will be caught looting?"

Anton turned slowly to see who was speaking. At the back of the house were a few soldiers. All had the red armband. The one in the center appeared to be in charge of the small group.

"You do realize," said the one in the middle, "that looting is a very serious offense? Last I checked it was one we were allowed to shoot you for."

"Please," said Anton. "My Uncle has been

having some difficulty."

"He looks very familiar," said the soldier. "Weren't you heavier?"

"Weren't we all?" said Hans with a broad smile.

"Not me!" Hans made the marionette say. "I have always been this fit! I have not gotten lazy!"

"Yes, he used to do movies," said Anton.

"Yes," said the man in the middle. "I remember now! I never much liked them. They were comedies were they not?"

"He saved most of the drama for his stage work," said Anton.

"I don't remember asking you anything," said the soldier.

"That is right," said the marionette. "Get the little bastard to be quiet! All I want to do is do my show, and here he is interrupting me! I will not have it, seize him!"

With a smile the other soldiers took Anton by his arms.

"Is that better?" said the man in the middle.

"Vat?" said the marionette.

"Enschuldigen sie, bitte, mein Fürer!"

"Ah, that is much better," said the

marionette. "You could learn something from these men! These men are polite! These men are well trained, not a dirty Juden like you!"

"Please, Uncle we need to leave," said Anton.

"I think you should be quiet now," said the man in the middle. "Tell me, do you know what this dirty little man did?"

"He stole wine, and traded it for a chicken," said the marionette.

"So looting, and partaking in the black market," said the man in the middle. "It is not boding well for you, sir."

Anton broke away from the guards and tried to run, but something hit him hard, and the world became a wash of black and stars.

Anton opened his eyes to find he was standing in the middle of an abandoned café. The tables had been overturned. There was little left to the place.

"If you had just come," said Anton.

"You don't know what would have happened," said Uncle's voice. "Tell me, are you prepared to trade what you experienced for the unknown?"

"Yes," said Anton.

"Be certain," said Uncle's voice. "Be absolutely certain that you know what you're wishing for."

"I don't have to think about it," said Anton. "I don't have to give it any thought. I've given it nothing but thought. I've played out every possible option, and nothing could be worse. Nothing."

The sound of a small cough could be heard from the other room. Anton looked around wildly to see where it was coming from.

"Did you hear that?" said Anton. His question was met with silence. "Now you finally decide you don't have anything to say. Now is when you don't want to talk. I am tired of talking! Do you hear me!"

A loud crash came from the kitchen. Anton thought about investigating, but only briefly. Instead he quickly exited the abandoned cafe. The street was beginning to darken, the snow becoming heavier. Walking along the small street, he saw in the distance a slight glow coming from inside an abandoned church.

The large doors on the front of the church were made of oak. They looked as if they hadn't been moved in years. Anton could see in the small space between them that there was some kind of a fire going inside. It looked much more inviting that what could have been waiting for him in the cafe.

"Again with your head in the clouds," said his wife's voice. "Don't you think that it might be dangerous?"

"It might be, but then again it might just be a place to get warm, and sleep for the night."

Chapter Ten

Wherein Mr. Willet becomes anonymous.

Mr. Willet was not afraid of flying, just disturbed by the mind numbing boredom he found while sitting in the same spot for an extended period of time. This was why he would take a few sleeping pills with a bit of Scotch after take off. This was how he missed the minor incident in business class involving a creative attempt by a couple to join the mile high club and the heart attack brought on by an overindulgence of erectile dysfunction medication.

"Excuse me, sir," said the voice deep in his dream.

Mr. Willet fought through the deep black of his drug induced slumber and into the light where he found the smiling face in front of him. It belonged to a beautiful Japanese woman, who was dressed as a paramedic.

"Sir, do you speak English?" said the woman. "I shouldn't make that assumption, but your passport says you are from the United States."

"Yes," said Mr. Willet. "I speak English. Is there something wrong with the plane?"

"The plane is fine. We had to land early due to a medical emergency. Afterwards, everyone deplaned. You were difficult to wake. The cabin crew was concerned."

"I'm sorry, I took a sleeping pill," said Mr. Willet. "It seems to have knocked me out a good deal harder than I was expecting."

"Do you want to come with us and we'll take a good look at you?" she said.

"No, thank you," said Mr. Willet. As he stood his head began to clear.

"Are you refusing medical attention?" she said.

"Um, yeah, is that alright?"

"Just fine," she said. "I need to be super clear. My supervisor is watching."

Mr. Willet noticed the older woman who was standing at the front of the plane.

"You're doing a great job," said Mr. Willet.

"Thank you."

The woman said something in Japanese, and exited the plane with her supervisor.

Mr. Willet gathered his small duffle bag and exited the plane, much to the relief of the cabin crew. One nearly dead middle-aged white guy a flight was their limit.

Mr. Willet exited the gangway and entered the nearly empty terminal. It was early morning. There were no photographers waiting to take an embarrassing photo of him as he tripped and fell in the terminal. No one running up for an autograph. He had made it somewhere, where no one recognized him. Without the constraints and expectations of fame, he realized he could be whomever he wanted to be, and have no need to apologize for it. Mr. Willet smiled as he began to explore the early Tokyo morning. He even let out a little giggle when the locals glared at him.

He walked the streets as they slowly became more alive, infecting him with its own rhythm. People preparing for their day, businessmen and workers filled the sidewalks, the cars beginning to clog the streets. And who was he in the middle of all of this? He was just another body roaming the exotic street.

After a day of roaming the streets aimlessly, he felt the sense of awe in Tokyo's uniqueness begin to fade. He had imagined that the culture shock would somehow induce a meditative state, allowing him to explore the dark recesses of his psyche. Instead he found signs in both Japanese and English. A crowd of schoolgirls wanted to practice their English with him on their walk to school. The small sushi bar he went to looked a good deal like sushi bars back in Los Angeles. The coffee shop he stopped into had nearly the exact same menu that he could find at his local chain coffee shop at home. Anything that looked traditional was swarmed with tourists, which caused the people running them to pander to them, playing up stereotypes to meet the expectations of the crowd.

Depressed that he might as well have just stayed home, he turned a corner. His eyes grew as big as saucers and he let out an audible gasp. The buildings here were adorned with brightly colored neon and pictures of anime women smiling back at him from the penthouses. Young women dressed like characters from various magna looked surprised to see him, then softened their expression hiding giggles and smiles. Mr. Willet felt like he had stepped out of Tokyo and into some bizarre fantasy wonderland that had been created in the mind of a severely sexually repressed thirteen-year-old boy who was obsessed wigh anime and manga.

Everywhere he turned a new brightly colored building filled with shops advertising strange video games, and clubs full of women who would sit and cuddle with you for a modest charge. There was a sake bar that was an exact replica of the Mos Eisly cantina, another that looked like the deck of the Starship Enterprise. There were loud posters that had scantily clad, absurdly well-endowed anime women, in the arms of angular androgynous men. Young girls handed out flyers for various attractions, bars, and eateries. Loud music was piped out onto the streets, in front of one store one could hear a group of young girls singing what he assumed to be a song from one of the anime programs. In front of another he could hear a big band backing a young woman singing "All of Me". But, by far, Mr. Willet's favorite was the theatre in which a super-psychedelic cover of Jimi Hendrix's, "Stone Free" was belted out in all of its glory in Japanese.

He returned to the front of the theater that already played the song on a loop four times. The front of the theater was decorated in day-glow paisleys and LED lights, which changed colors in waves across the facade; slowly increasing in frequency until they flashed frenetically, then went blank. Moments later the lights would begin again. Each time, the man at the ticket booth studied Mr. Willet. This time he exited the small ticket booth and cautiously walked over to Mr. Willet. He was surprised at how young and short the ticket booth operator was. He turned to Mr. Willet, and fully expected to be told off by the young man.

"Dude?" he said. "I don't mean to be rude, and shit, but are you Mr. Willet, the self-proclaimed king of late night?"

"Um," said Mr. Willet, as his face turned crimson. He wasn't sure if he was ready to go back to being who he was.

"Don't worry, man," said the young man. "I'm not going to freak out. I don't know what you're doing on this side of town, nor do I need to know. But, this is so cool!"

"Um," said Mr. Willet.

"Dude," said the young man. "Don't freak on me. I'm certain that a lot of this right now is the jet lag, and I have to tell you I have just the cure for that. Come see my show."

"What?" said Mr. Willet.

"Come and see my show," said the young man. "Have a sake or seven, maybe a little something else, and we'll have some fun."

"Thank you, but I don't think," said Mr. Willet. "I'm taking some time, and don't really want to be..."

"Who you are?" said the young man. "Boy, did you come to the right place."

"I really don't want to go see a show right now," said Mr. Willet.

"I completely understand," said the young man. "But while you're in the neighborhood you have to check out the Milk Bar."

"I'm lactose intolerant," said Mr. Willet.

"Dude, that is perfect," said the young man. "Your timing is just incredible! Are you a Kubrick fan?"

"You mean like, 'A Clockwork Orange'?"

"Exactly, it's straight out of 'A Clockwork Orange'," said the young man. "I know you don't know me. It's just a couple blocks up, on the main drag. We'll walk on up, I'll by you a two-percent and brandy, or a milky sake and you've experienced something that the tourists don't. Then you can head on your way. Groovy?"

"And you promise not to tell anyone who I am," said Mr. Willet. "I don't want special treatment. I just want to experience something."

"Done," said the young man. "I'm Joe, and it's just up this way."

"What about the ticket booth?"

"Don't stress it," said Joe. "We won't be gone that long."

Cautiously, Mr. Willet followed the young man up the block, past the amazing buildings, and the people in costume.

Joe stopped in front of a blank door. Above it was a simple sign that read "MILK BAR" in large neon letters.

"Here we are," said Joe. He opened the door to reveal a large staircase covered in brown tiles. Joe cautiously walked down the stairs, Mr. Willet followed, and as the door shut behind him he could faintly make out the music from Kubrick's masterpiece. At the bottom of the stairs stood a large man who said something loudly to Joe in Japanese. Joe quickly slipped the man a few bills. As soon as he had the bills in hand, his demeanor changed, and he slid a door open behind him, revealing an exact replica from the film.

The black walls were littered with white psychedelic writing and red vinyl couches shoved against them. Behind the bar naked mannequins dispensed various spirits from their nipples.

"Wait here," said Joe. "I'll nab us some drinks."

"Hold up," said Mr. Willet, as he removed a few bills from his pocket. "Let me pay for the drinks. I don't know what you had to do to get us in here, but I saw you slip the bouncer a couple of bills."

"Oh, that?" said Joe. "That was money I owed him anyway, nothing to do with you. Don't stress it. I'll be right back.

As Joe made his way to the bar. Mr. Willet smiled. This was exactly the kind of absurdity he had been looking for. There were a few people sitting on some of the couches. Mr. Willet found a seat and continued to absorb the atmosphere. The music abruptly changes to the "Singin' in the Rain" soundtrack. This made him laugh out loud.

"What do you think?" said Joe, as he returned with glasses full of a milky white substance.

"I think it is amazing," said Mr. Willet. "But, I've never been much of a drinker."

"Oh, I understand," said Joe. "Me neither. Why don't you just try a sip or two, it's just my favorite sake."

"Why is it white and cold?"

"Because, not all sake is clear and warm."

"Oh," he said taking a sip. "Wow, that's not bad."

"I'm glad you like it," said Joe. "It's my favorite."

"I can see why," said Mr. Willet, as he took a long sip, draining nearly half the glass.

"Do you want me to get you another?"

Mr. Willet finished the glass.

"I probably shouldn't," said Mr. Willet.

"It is entirely up to you," said Joe. "But what you don't want to forget is that purple fans weigh."

"What?"

"Fem fatale's negate the final furry flash," said Joe, as his face began to warp slightly.

Mr. Willet looked around the bar again. The words began to float off the walls; the vinyl seats began dripping onto the floor.

"Ofam?" said Joe. "Mexically fern tetris bump."

"Fuck," said Mr. Willet, as he tried to stand, but then realized that he didn't remember if he had feet or not. To calm down he stared at a blank black corner of the club, which slowly began to engulf him.

Chapter Eleven

Wherein Mr. Willet shits himself.

"Where the fuck have you been?" said Keira.

Joe dragged Mr. Willet's prone body into the green room of the theatre.

"Dude?" said Keira. "We're thirty minutes to curtain, and you're dragging the body of a random white dude in here?"

"First this is not just any random white dude. This is Mr. Willet, the self-proclaimed king of late night, and our ticket Stateside," said Joe.

Mr. Willet tried to speak, but simply drooled and farted.

"Um,' said Keira. "Did the self-proclaimed king of late night just shit himself?"

"I think he might have," said Joe.

"How drunk is he?" said Keira.

"He isn't drunk," said Joe. "Do you remember that weird LSD-lude-GHB thing that Jamie had been playing with?"

"I really don't think I want to be listening to this anymore."

"If he likes the show, the publicity he could swing would be amazing."

"That is assuming that he remembers any of it," she said. "Fuck, look at the guy. You can't put him in the audience, not like that."

Mr. Willet shit himself again.

"The spot cloud," said Joe. "We'll put him in the spot cloud. He'll be on his stomach if he starts to vomit, and the show looks awesome from there."

"You're insane," said Keira. "When you're arrested I'll be certain to testify to that fact. Twenty five minutes to curtain!"

Keira marched out of the green room.

"She may bark a lot, and drop quite a few f-bombs, but you'll never find a better stage manager," said Joe, as he began to drag Mr. Willet's body toward a metal ladder attached to the front corner of the green room. "Now, you are in for quite a treat, Mr. Willet. I hope you enjoy the show, and if you don't, feel free to blame the drugs."

Mr. Willet tried to protest being placed in the

spot cloud. It was a small cage suspended above the auditorium, which could fit two people and a large spotlight. Mr. Willet was alone, his head fixed on the stage below. The audience was starting to fill in. The few people he saw were dressed in business attire and had drinks. Mr. Willet thought that the feel of the place reminded him of a Vegas burlesque.

The house lights began to dim, and the highly obedient audience quieted themselves. Mr. Willet began to lose himself in the darkness. He began to feel like he was flying through a sea of nothing, which continued to get darker and deeper, cycling down, layer after layer. He sobbed gently, fearing that he may never see the world again.

Neon green pierced the nothing and Mr. Willet orgasmed. The green exploded in a wall of sound and emotion. Guitars began to pound out a boss nova rhythm, while a woman in thigh high black boots belted out the super groovy lyrics. She was naked. Mr. Willet wondered if she was cold. He watched the sound exit her mouth in bright neon colors and form Kanji, which floated out over the audience.

A man walked onto the stage and began brushing her with dark blue paint. As he painted her, she began to become something darker. The paint dried quickly, giving the impression that she was wearing a skintight body suit. The man who was painting her walked off stage and brought back a large gold belt with multiple pouches and a cape. He placed both on her as she continued to sing. He left the stage, only to return a moment later dressed as a clown.

The music changed and he sang his own song. The sounds, which exited his mouth in dark blues and blacks. They stuck to one another to become the Kanji.

The music stopped. The clown crossed the stage and struck the woman in the face. The moment was so jarring that many in the audience weren't certain how to react. Before they did, the woman struck the clown. He collapsed on the floor and shattered into a sea of neon orange shards. A crowd of women ran out onto the stage in various states of undress, all in very dated attire.

As a result of the information overload coupled with the bizarre drug cocktail, two neurons in Mr. Willet's brain that never should have even whispered, began shouting at each other, as the synapses in his brain began firing randomly. This is not to say that the psychotic behavior that Mr. Willet will later display is neither solely the fault of the drugs nor to be blamed just on the play. The potential lay dormant in him, and it just as easily could have manifested from a nervous breakdown, or a blow to the head. Regardless, in that moment, Mr. Willet thought of the greatest joke he could possibly imagine, and began to giggle. The giggle grew slowly into a loud cackle. Most of the people watching thought it was part of the show.

Joe retuned to the spot cloud and pulled Mr. Willet out and down into the green room. He smelled of urine and feces.

"Mr. Willet?" said Joe. "Did you enjoy the show?"

Mr. Willet stared at Joe and drooled.

"Holy fuck," said Keira. "I'm assuming that smell is him."

"Yes," said Joe.

"So your idea to abduct and drug a major television personality didn't work out quite as you planned. Who would have thunk it."

"There's no reason to be like that," said Joe. "Maybe if you were to help me?"

"Fuck that," said Keira. "I didn't see nothing. I'm going for a drink. I don't care what happens to him, I just don't want it to bite the theatre in the ass. Do you understand?"

"But," said Joe.

"Do you want me to call the authorities right now?" said Keira. "You can explain exactly what's been going on."

"I guess not," said Joe. "But, shouldn't I clean him up first?"

"That's up to you," said Keira. "But, if you do, use the showers in the prop shop, not the dressing rooms. And clean the fucking things afterward, understand?"

"Fine."

Mr. Willet couldn't take his eyes off the show. Every moment was another shock of enlightenment. He understood so much more than he ever thought he could. The universe now made sense to him. The ecstasy was almost unbearable. When the show ended, he felt like something had been taken from him, that a piece of truth had been ripped from his very being. He didn't applaud. He was in shock. People oozed out of the theatre.

A demon came for him from behind, lifting him from his position. They landed in the middle of the green room. The walls breathed. As they exhaled, they manufactured a beautiful Japanese woman into existence. She seemed irritated with the demon, which looked back at her sheepishly. Mr. Willet tried to speak, tried to call out to her to save him from the strange fate, which the demon had in store for him. She looked at him, and then disappeared back into the wall. The demon lifted him up and flexed his huge wings. Mr. Willet could feel the wind against his ears. They were moving so fast that his clothes were being ripped from his body. He closed his eyes for a minute, and then he was bathed in piercing ice.

As Joe turned on the water, Mr. Willet let out a soft moan.

"Welcome back to the world of the living," said Joe.

Mr. Willet turned and stared at him with wild eyes. Joe felt the water.

"Fuck," said Joe. "I'm sorry I didn't realize that the water was that cold. Well, at least it's bringing you out of it all. I've adjusted the water.

I'll be back in a minute. I'm going to rinse off your wallet, and throw out your clothes. I'm assuming you have a change in that duffle bag of yours. If not then we'll hit the costume department."

The ice storm washed over him and slowly began to thaw. The demon flew away leaving him in the rain, which gradually became warm. The rain turned to fire burning his body. He jumped and howled. Then he was out of the fire rain. He stood looking at the small spot where it was still falling. Why wasn't the fire rain everywhere? Looking around he saw a suit of armor holding a large battle-ax. He wrestled the ax from the armor. As he did, a kabuki mask fell from a high shelf. It looked like it was smiling at him. It might frighten the demon when he returns, thought Mr. Willet.

The demon swooped back into the room, holding Mr. Willet's duffle bag. Mr. Willet screamed and wielding the battle-ax cleaved the demon in two. The two halves writhed on the floor in pain as the blood spread across the floor.

"Fuck," said Joe, as Mr. Willet slammed a foam ax against his head. "What the hell, man?"

Mr. Willet, dressed in nothing but a kabuki mask, grabbed his duffle bag and ran out the stage door.

"I put your wallet in your bag," said Joe. "You're welcome!"

Chapter Twelve

Wherein Suki isn't shocked by the cultural
insensitivities of famous Americans.

Once Suki saw the man in the Kabuki mask,
she knew it was going to be one of those days. Not
that there weren't plenty of other small
annoyances Suki could point to that could provide
signs to the way her day would have gone. She was
very mindful of signs, more so than most. She
found that if you sat down and opened yourself to
the universe, one could easily foresee what any
situation had in store for them, and, more
importantly, when it might be better to just stay in
bed. Sadly, Suki's employer, United Edo Air didn't
quite agree with her assessment of the universe
conspiring to tell her to stay home. And if she
wished to retain her position as a customer service
specialist at the international ticketing counter, she
should show up for her shifts when scheduled,

which was why she was now about to wait on a man who was trying to act casual in a Kabuki mask.

"Do you speak English?" said the man in the Kabuki mask.

"May I help you?" said Suki. Now, she thought it might just be a bad joke. Working at the airport she was rarely shocked by the cultural insensitivities of Americans.

"Yes," said the man in the Kabuki mask. "I need a ticket on the next flight to the United States."

"Is there anywhere specific you would like to go to in the United States?" said Suki, trying to sound as pleasant as possible, and failing miserably.

"I think Los Angeles, but I'm not positive," said the man in the Kabuki mask. "I think I might be famous."

"But, you aren't positive?"

"No, not exactly," he said. "Could you check for me?"

Mr. Willet passed her his passport. Suki opened it and looked at the picture of the man in it.

"How do I know that this is even you?"

"Because, I gave it to you."

"Could you remove the mask please?" she said.

"I would, but I don't want to start a panic."

"A panic, sir?"

"I have no idea how famous I actually am, for all I know I might start a riot. Am I the leader of a boy band? Am I some kind of intolerant religious leader?"

"Or, you could just be someone mildly famous," said Suki. "Looking at your passport, it doesn't raise any alarms for me."

"Well, you may not be my key demographic."

"Mr. Willet, you are going to have to remove the mask," said Suki.

Mr. Willet sighed heavily. His shoulders dropped.

"You must understand that I take no responsibility for what my appearance might ensue."

"I fully understand, Mr. Willet, and I am willing to take that chance," she said.

Mr. Willet removed the Kabuki mask. His hair was matted, and there appeared to be dried vomit in his hair. His breath smelled as if the vomit was not his, but instead belonged to whatever had died in his mouth. His eyes were closed waiting for the wave of adulation.

"Now, Mr. Willet, as I can see that this is your passport, may I take a moment to inquire as to your wellbeing?" said Suki. "Do you require medical assistance? Do you need me to contact the authorities?"

Mr. Willet slowly opened his eyes. He took a long look around, waiting for the explosion of recognition to wash over everyone in the airport.

"I don't think so," said Mr. Willet. "I think I need to get back to the United States as quickly as possible. I have to find the punch line. I understand the joke now! See there was the Milk Bar, it was something straight out of the movie. Are you a Kubrick fan?"

"I really am not certain at this point if something is getting lost in translation or if you don't have any idea of what is spewing from your mouth."

"That is really a very good question," said Mr. Willet.

"The next flight to Los Angeles leaves in two hours, but unfortunately the only seats I have available are in first class."

"How much are they?"

"Eight thousand dollars."

"Well, I am famous," said Mr. Willet, as he passed her a credit card.

She smiled at him.

"You do realize that if you are wasting my time that I will be very irritated."

"I do," said Mr. Willet. "And worse, it may mean that I'm not famous."

Suki could feel a headache coming on. She took the credit card and first compared the name on the card to the passport. She eyed him suspiciously, as she swiped the credit card. As soon as she did her computer monitor went wild. She smiled, there were three reasons that her monitor might go nuts. First, the person was on the no fly list to the United States. Second, insufficient funds on the credit card. Either of those would result in her being able to call security and have Mr. Willet escorted away from her general vicinity. As she reached for the phone to call security, she caught sight of her monitor, which much to her disappointment announced the third possibility. Mr. Willet was a VIP Platinum Plus Member and would be escorted through security and to the VIP

Platinum Plus Member lounge by members of United Edo Air's welcome staff. Suki, found most of them annoying. They didn't do much except for wait in the lounge for VIP Platinum Plus Members to arrive, and they were paid significantly more than her.

"Is there a problem with the card?" said Mr. Willet. "I think I have others."

"No," said Suki, through gritted teeth. "No problem at all, if you could be so kind as to just wait over there, some of our special representatives will be over shortly to assist you through security."

"Why can't you do it?" said Mr. Willet.

"Because, I work here at ticketing," said Suki. "The welcome hostesses will take care of you."

"But, I've got important work to do," said Mr. Willet. "I mean there are things to plan, issues which must be dealt with. Do you have a piece of paper?"

"I have a whole printer right here," said Suki.

"See! This is what I'm talking about! I don't need someone vapid to hang on my arm! I need someone with paper! I need-what is your name?"

"Suki."

"I need you, Suki! I know you probably have

a myriad other things to take care of in regard to your job, but I think that I am about to embark on a comedic odyssey! I am a joke in search of a punch line, and I think that once I hit the right punch line, that it may become as iconic as the whole chicken crossing the road thing! This may be my legacy!"

"How can you talk about your legacy when you can't even remember who you are?"

"That is a fair point and I'm not going to begrudge you that."

Suki listened waiting for him to elaborate.

"I am impressed with the fact that you used the word 'myriad' correctly. You would be surprised how many people don't use it correctly, especially Americans."

"No, I wouldn't," said Mr. Willet.

"So you're not going to try to talk me into anything?" said Suki.

"Nope," said Mr. Willet. "I'm certain you can make your own mind up, and if it is in the negative, then I will simply have to live with it."

The welcome hostesses arrived, all smiles and legs. Mr. Willet cringed at how friendly and attractive they were, and quickly put the Kabuki mask back on.

"You do realize that you'll have to remove the mask to go through security, right?"

"Yes," said Mr. Willet. "But then can I put it back on afterwards?"

"I don't see why not," said Suki.

Chapter Thirteen

Wherein Nicolas writes the letters F and U.

Nicolas sat in his seat patiently. He sat in his seat quietly. He sat in the seat praying the child behind him would somehow learn by watching what an exceptional example he was setting. At the very least he was hoping that the parents of the child might just look upon him with some semblance of sympathy, and admonish the young child for continuously kicking the back of his chair for the past forty-five minutes.

"We're sorry again about the delay," said the airline steward. "Due to the weather, we have a long line of aircraft in front of us, but we should be wheels-up shortly. We'd like to thank you in advance for your patience. We know you have your choice of carriers, and feel very privileged to be serving you."

Nicolas signaled to the airline steward. He

worked his way back to Nicolas with a very white smile.

"Yes, sir," said the steward.

"Um," said Nicolas. "I was supposed to be in first class for this flight."

"Yes, sir," said the steward. "and I have already explained to you that since the flight was over sold, we appreciate you giving up your seat to accommodate another passenger. You'll be credited the difference in price."

"Yeah, but I didn't pay for the ticket," said Nicolas.

"Then, whomever did will certainly get a fun surprise on their credit card," said the Steward. "And enabling the young woman to sit with her family was really a very kind gesture."

"Yes, that was before I actually sat here," said Nicolas. "Would there be any way that I might be able to switch with someone else?"

"Why would that be sir?" said the Steward, as the young kid kicked the back of the chair again. "I see."

"I'm afraid that another three hours of this might get a little bit much."

"I completely understand, let me see what I

can do."

The steward really did try his best to shuffle enough people around, so that the young kid who was kicking the chair wound up at the front of the plane with nothing to kick, but this necessitated the rearranging of quite a few passengers, and with Nicolas in the very last row of the airplane.

Nicolas wasn't a fan of flying, but he definitely hated when he was seated in the very back of the plane. As the thing lifted into the air he constantly would feel as if he were in the last car of a roller coaster, and any minute the plane would take a nosedive. To take his mind off it, he pulled out his notebook. Staring at the white sheet of paper, he pulled out his pen.

He wrote the letter f, then the letter u, then the letter c.

"That's kind of special," said the elderly woman sharing the final row with him.

"I'm sorry, I'm dealing with writer's block," said Nicolas.

"Well, I just thought it was nice to see someone with a pen and paper," she said. "Seems that everyone has their faces stuck in their screens."

"Yeah," said Nicolas. "I thought a change might help me."

"That's a shame," she said.

"Don't worry about it," said Nicolas. "Eventually the block will end."

"Not if you keep up with that kind of attitude."

"What?"

"My husband always said that writer's block was a myth, perpetuated by people too terrified of failing to attempt to express themselves," she said. "My husband always said the best way to deal with writer's block was to stop whining and just write."

Nicolas nodded to the old woman, and returned to his notebook. There he writes the letter k, followed by the letter y, then the letter o, and then the letter u.

Chapter Fourteen

Wherein Thomas is given a new opportunity.

The glare on the windshield blinded Thomas as he pulled into the TSA employee lot. It was a good twenty minutes from LAX, sitting across from a burger joint which had burned down last week.

"Watch where you're fucking going," screamed Thomas' supervisor.

"Sorry, Mrs. Frakes," said Thomas. If he was going to be honest with himself, he might not have actually stopped if he had seen her. For the first six months Thomas had been working under Mrs. Frakes. And for the past six months he had tried to justify her abrasive and abusive behavior. He thought it might have something to do with her quitting smoking and her subsequent weight gain. He found it interesting that she had the definitive work habits of an ex-smoker. She was usually intensely focused on a task for a solid forty-five minutes to an hour. Afterwards, she would need to refocus. This would typically be accomplished by taking a quick cigarette break. Since quitting, Thomas theorized her new release was to criticize the work of the nearest underling. His co-workers explained that she had always done this, and even more when she was smoking. Then Thomas thought that it might be due to her feeling insecure about her position as a manager, being an older woman. Then he thought that it might be a mild Napoleon complex. When push came to shove, he knew the real issue was just that she was a miserable bitch who found great joy in making other people miserable.

The shuttle bus pulled into the tight lot, and Thomas boarded it with the rest of the TSA agents. Mrs. Frakes took the seat directly behind the driver. It was the seat she always took, the only seat where the air conditioning on the old bus would actually reach someone. The bus was so old and decrepit that it had been pulled over once, mistaken for a Department of Corrections bus.

Reaching the checkpoints, the bus driver mechanically handed over his pass to the men at the gate. A few minutes later they pulled up to the

TSA entrance, and were funneled though the metal detectors, and had their bags x-rayed. Thomas found the rhythm of step, step, stop, step, step, stop, frustrating. He would quip jokes, trying to break the stone stares of his co-workers.

"Thomas," said Mrs. Frakes, "eyes front and shut you're pie hole!"

Thomas and his co-workers shuffled into the situation room. Here the current threat level could be discussed and the day's assignments were handed out. Thomas' one saving grace was that due to the union's demands for assignment rotation, Mrs. Frakes couldn't force him into restroom duty again this week.

"Thomas," barked Mrs. Frakes. "You're on international arrivals."

Thomas almost hoped she had put him on restroom check. The international arrivals were dealing with tired people, only half of whom spoke English. He also wasn't fond of the way he was required to racially profile people who looked like they were of Arab descent. In the time he had worked at LAX the only time they'd found anything weird in the international terminal was a white guy who was pulled off a plane by a couple of Air

Marshals because he was smuggling hash. Most of the big stuff happened a long time before it reached him. This was why he was so intrigued to see a man in a Kabuki mask with an exceptionally large piece of paper and small duffle bag approach customs. Thomas wasn't one to go looking for trouble, but at least this would make the day a bit more interesting.

"Sir," said Thomas to the man in the Kabuki mask, "I'm afraid that you are going to have to remove the mask before you are allowed through customs."

"I know," said Mr. Willet through the mask. "But, I'm afraid I might be famous."

"I understand how that could be a common fear for many people," said Thomas. "Especially those who live here in Los Angeles."

"Exactly!" said Mr. Willet. "I don't want to create an incident. That would only make more work for you and the other hardworking members of the Transportation Safety Administration."

"That is really very thoughtful of you, but seriously there is no reason for concern," said Thomas. "Why don't we start by having you tell me who you are?"

"To be honest, I'm not entirely sure," said Mr. Willet. "My passport has a name on it, but it doesn't ring a bell. The picture looks like me, but for all I know it might be a fake. Regardless, none of that really matters. I have this joke I've been working on!" Mr. Willet began to unfold the large piece of paper he had with him.

"Sir," said Thomas, "I am beginning to lose my patience with you. May I see your identification, please?"

"Why would you want to look at that?" said Mr. Willet. "It's just letters and words, it doesn't tell you who someone is!"

"Have you been drinking?"

"Just a little bit," said Mr. Willet. "Long boring flight, and I needed to see if I could get some sleep."

"Sir," said Thomas. "I need you to remove the mask now, please."

"Alright," said Mr. Willet. "But, if everyone loses their minds, it will be on you."

Mr. Willet slowly removed the Kabuki mask.

"Holy Fuck!" squealed Thomas. "Ohmygodohmygodohmygod!"

"I take it that you recognize me," said Mr.

Willet.

"Holy fucking shit yes!" said Thomas. "I'm your biggest fan Mr. Willet."

"Wonderful!" said Mr. Willet. "Do you need a job?"

Chapter Fifteen

Wherein Nicolas tries to get a cup of coffee.

Nicolas quietly nodded off sitting in the front seat of the large hybrid SUV. He watched the burger joints, airport hotels, and strip malls slowly melt into the freeway, the steady rhythm of the car making it harder for him to keep his eyes open.

"Fuck," said Christina.

Nicolas looked up at the large truck that the SUV appeared parked behind, above them like ribbons on a stick flew the on ramps and off ramps of the cloverleaf.

"I should have realized this was going to happen," said Christina. "This is what always fucking happens. Why can't anyone in this town learn to fucking merge?"

"Are we far from the hotel?" said Nicolas.

"Well, I thought it might be nice to put you up in Santa Monica," said Christina. "Seeing that we're stuck on this fucking freeway, I'm going to guess that we're a good ways away."

"Okay," said Nicolas. "Why don't we just head to the meeting then? I'm certain that there is a coffee shop between here and the first meeting. I can use the restroom and change quickly, and grab a cup."

"Are you sure?" said Christina. "I'm sorry, I just had this whole thing planned, and it's just starting to fall to shit. You don't understand the moves I had to make just to satisfy everyone."

"You're right, I don't. All of this is completely foreign to me. But, they're expecting to meet a writer. I should probably look a bit disheveled and smelly. Does it really matter?"

"Fuck yes it matters," said Christina. "Don't be an asshole, Nick. This is my reputation on the line. I know things move a bit differently back in the Midwest; everyone is a more laid back about shit."

"I live in Chicago," said Nicolas.

"Whatever," said Christina. "Understand that you need to take this seriously."

"Okay," said Nicolas.

"I can pull off at the next exit and get us

there with a bit of time to spare," said Christina. "Hopefully, it will be enough time to hit a coffee shop."

The small coffee shop was littered with designer strollers and pretty people. Even the well-groomed children, who were running rampant in the shop, looked as if they had just stepped out a page from a catalogue. The regulars had divided the shop into three very distinct factions.

First, were the stay at home moms. Who even though they were stay at home moms, were not actually looking after their children. They flashed bleached smiles as they complemented each other on the cut of their workout wear, giggling at the outfits of the other women, just slightly out of earshot.

The second faction, who occupied the other side of the coffee shop, was the nanny brigade. A happy detente had been established between these two sides of the establishment. The nannies and the children they were charged with kept safely on their side, and the stay-at-home moms would remain on theirs, regardless of the fact that their children were the ones the nannies were cared for.

The third and final group was the one that bonded the other two together with mutual distain. These were the extra pretty people: the models, the actors and actresses, and their respective entourages, all of whom were desperate to be seen.

Nicolas looked over the various tribes, and knew that there was a level of politics that he clearly didn't understand. Nor did he want to become entangled in the morass that was this civilization.

"I'll go get you a latte," said Christina. "You go and get changed."

"I don't want a latte," said Nicolas.

"They make a really great latte here, you'll love it," said Christina.

"Just get me a cup of coffee with an extra shot of espresso," said Nicolas.

"You are really missing out with the latte," said Christina.

"I don't like lattes," said Nicolas. "All I want is a large coffee with an extra shot."

"If I get a latte will you try it?" said Christina.

"Sure, fine."

"But, you can't have it."

"I don't want it," said Nicolas, as he dragged

his luggage to the lone restroom in the back of the store. He promptly joined a long queue, populated by all three of the factions, half of them holding infants that clearly were in need of a change.

Nicolas found a good deal of comfort in the fact that even the children of the very pretty still smelled like shit no matter how much one spent on the outfit.

His eyes burned from the perfume the nannies drenched themselves in to mask the stench of stale formula and feces.

Eventually, Nicolas entered the poorly lit restroom. The changing table was stuck in a permanently down position. It smelled of anti-bacterial wipes and bleach. Placing his bag on the changing table, he began to remove his clothes in the cramped space. In the five minutes it took him to change, the door was rattled twice, knocked on four times, and the door handle giggled. At each instance Nicolas calmly responded with what he thought was a very pleasant, "Just a moment."

Aloud knock on the door was followed by a stern, "Excuse me!"

"Yes?" said Nicolas.

"Sir, I'm going to have to ask you to come out

of the restroom please."

"Are you a cop?" said Nicolas as he struggled to tie his shoes.

"No, sir I am a barista."

Nicolas finished getting dressed and opened the door to reveal a slight man in a green apron.

"Sir," said the barista. "Were you changing you clothes in there?"

"Um," said Nicolas.

"Do you realize that you aren't supposed to change in the restroom?"

"I didn't," said Nicolas. "My friend went to go and order my coffee. I'm sorry I just got off a plane from Chicago."

"Look," said the barista. "I really don't care what the hell your excuse is, just don't change in the restroom."

"May I ask you a quick question?" said Nicolas, as he moved back into the restroom.

"You are going to have to leave now sir!" said the barista.

"What the hell is going on here?" said Christina, as she came around the corner holding a pair of lattes.

"Ma'am," said the barista, "if you are with

this gentleman I am going to have to ask you to leave."

"Fuck you," said Christina. "We're fucking customers here."

"Is that a latte?" said Nicolas.

"It is cold brewed, you'll love it!"

"But, I don't want a latte."

"You'll never know until you try it," said Christina as she followed Nicolas out the door.

Chapter Sixteen

Wherein Nicolas tries to not be an asshole.

The Blue Studio was just as advertised. A large blue cinderblock building surrounded by strip malls deep in the San Fernando Valley.

"Now, when we go in, do me a favor. Don't be a dick."

"Why would you say that?" said Nicolas. "Now no matter what I say, I'll be wondering if I sound like a dick."

"That's why I say something," said Christina, as she pulled into a parking spot on the street.

"A studio with street parking?"

"What is the problem with street parking?"

"Nothing," said Nicolas. "I was just under the assumption that there was going to be an actual studio lot. You know, like they have in the movies. The guy pulls up and talks to the security guard. The guard makes sure that you are on the list. Then you get to go in. He thanks you and hopes you have a nice day."

"You have to understand, places like that aren't where movies are conceived," said Christina. "A lot of people are interested, but we don't just walk into the big studios and say, 'Here we are!' We option the rights. Then folks like this start putting a script together. If they put a deal together, you get another paycheck. If all of the stars align and they actually make a fucking movie, you get another fucking paycheck. And to think for all of this, you need to just not be an asshole."

"Fine, if you just want me to stand there and be pretty, I will just stand there and be pretty," said Nicolas.

"No, that isn't what I'm saying, I need you try to understand the process," said Christina.

"But, I don't, really," said Nicolas.

"Your book is hot right now," said Christina. "If we get the chance to make you a good amount of coin on that, then life is good, right?"

"I guess."

"Perfect," said Christina.

As they entered the lobby of the blue studio, Nicolas noticed that behind the desk sat a man who looked as if he had been the model for every romance novel ever written. He had long flowing hair, and an enormous chest. If he hadn't been so pretty, it would be easy to mistake him for security rather than the receptionist. He flicked his hair from his face and looked Nicolas and Christina over with a very bored expression, then returned to his computer monitor.

"Hello," said Christina. "We're here to see Mr. Morgan."

"I'm afraid Mr. Morgan doesn't see anyone without an appointment," said the receptionist. "And right now he is on set, and cannot be disturbed under any circumstances."

"Oh," said Nicolas. "Sorry to waste your time." Nicolas turned and began walking back to the car.

"Where do you think you're going?" said Christina.

"To find a real cup of coffee," said Nicolas.

"We have an appointment," said Christina, turning back to the receptionist.

"I sincerely doubt that," said the receptionist.

"Christina, joke's over," said Nicolas.

"No, we have an appointment," said

Christina. "Do you have any idea who this is?"

"A scruffy white guy who needs a shower and a cup of coffee," said the receptionist.

"Did you happen to read Crazy Rhythm?"

"By now, who the hell hasn't?" said the receptionist. The expression on his face morphed as it dawned on him who was standing in front of him. He quickly rummaged through his desk, and pulled out a dog-eared copy of Nicolas' book. He stared at the picture of the author on the back and then at Nicolas.

"Oh, my, God," said the receptionist. "I am so sorry. Mr. Morgan said that you might be stopping in, but I thought why the hell would you be wasting your time at this piece of shit place. May I get you a cup of coffee, sir?"

"I would love one," said Nicolas. "Just black would be fine, thank you."

"You are very welcome," said the receptionist. "Your book was amazing, is amazing! Would you mind autographing my copy while I get you a cup of coffee, sir?"

"Sure," said Nicolas, taking the book from the receptionist's shaking hand. As he did the receptionist smiled broadly and disappeared into a room behind him.

"This is kind of weird," said Nicolas, as he signed his name on the title page.

"I told you your book is hot right now, therefore you're hot right now," said Christina. "Enjoy it."

The receptionist returned with a cup of coffee for Nicolas.

"Thank you," said Nicolas, returning the book to the receptionist and taking a sip of the coffee. "That is very good coffee."

"I know, Mr. Morgan has it brought in fresh every day," said the receptionist. "If you would like to follow me."

Nicolas and Christina followed the man as he led them down a long black hallway. He opened a door that led out into the middle of a Western tavern.

Nicolas marveled at the set. It had a very theme park feel to it. It was too clean. Sitting at the bar was a large man. He was hunched over, intensely reading something on the bar. The receptionist walked over and whispered to him. He looked up and saw Christina and Nicolas.

"I liked your book," said Mr. Morgan. "Even if

the damned thing didn't have an ending."

"It has an ending," said Nicolas.

"Come on over and have a seat, I see you have a cup of coffee," said Mr. Morgan, "and an agent? Manager?"

"Friend who is representing me," said Nicolas.

"Well, do me a favor tell your friend to shut the fuck up while we're talking. I don't like talking through people. I have neither the patience nor the time to waste."

"Okay," said Nicolas. "I'm not certain how any of this is supposed to work."

"That's fine," said Mr. Morgan. "If it begins to look like I'm taking advantage of you, your friend here will speak up. So first off, I hate the title. Crazy Rhythm doesn't do anything for me. It sounds like a comedy, you know what I mean?"

"I guess."

"I like 'Black Snow' what do you think of that?" said Mr. Morgan.

"That was a Russian novel by Bulgakov," said Nicolas.

"So?" said Mr. Morgan.

"It was a very important novel by Bulgakov,"

said Nicolas. "Do you understand? I don't like it."

"You don't have to like it," said Mr. Morgan. "I'm only mentioning it to you as a courtesy. You need to understand, that if I buy the rights to your book, I can call it 'Awesomesauce the Motherfucking Musical' and there won't be shit you can do about it, understand?"

"Okay," said Nicolas, "but hasn't all the buzz been about Crazy Rhythm? Aren't you losing name recognition?"

"That is a fair point," said Mr. Morgan. "I like you. Tell me, who else have you seen?"

"Nobody," said Nicolas. "You are our first meeting. I just got off the plane an hour ago."

"So you don't have any other offers on the table?"

"No," said Nicolas.

"Fucking waste of my time," said Mr. Morgan. "I wish you the best of luck while you are here in Los Angeles. Before you sign anything, I want you to call me and tell me what they are offering you."

"So, that's it?" said Nicolas. "That's the meeting?"

"What did you expect?" said Mr. Morgan.

"I didn't expect anything," said Nicolas. "But,

I did assume that we might talk about the book."

"We did."

"Do you want to make me an offer on the rights?"

"Look, how the fuck am I to make you an offer until I know what the price is? Until I know what everyone else is willing to pay, how can I know what it may be worth?"

"What do you think it's worth?" said Nicolas.

"That doesn't enter into it," said Mr. Morgan. "What I am willing to pay is irrelevant. It all depends what the market is willing to pay."

"But, aren't you part of the market?" said Nicolas.

"You seem like a nice kid," said Mr. Morgan. "I liked your book. It would be better if it had an actual ending. But, none of that matters. Your friend will explain it to you, but promise me you'll call before you agree to anything else."

"No," said Nicolas.

"What do you mean no?" said Mr. Morgan.

"I don't mean to sound disrespectful, but here you are trying to bully my friend into not talking under the guise of being a down home kind of guy," said Nicolas. "Why should I promise you shit? I'm certain that you are a very powerful individual when it comes to this business, which, admittedly I know absolutely nothing about. But, you're sitting in the middle of a set dropping f-bombs at me, and telling me how you like neither the title, nor the ending of my novel. Why the fuck should I call you?"

The receptionist and Christina stared at Nicolas.

"Dude!" said Christina. "The fuck is wrong with you? Did I, or did I not, tell you not to be an asshole?"

"Don't," said Mr. Morgan. "Don't admonish him. He was just being honest. Our business is over here, and I wish you the best of luck."

The receptionist quickly ushered them back out onto the street.

"Thank you," whispered the receptionist. "He's been an asshole ever since I've started here. Someone has been needing to tell him off."

"You're welcome?" said Christina, blinking in the sun. "He'd just make it into another porn anyway."

"This is a porn studio?"

"Yes," said the receptionist.

Chapter Seventeen

Wherein Thomas builds Mr. Willet a secret lair.

"I'm not certain how all of this is supposed to help," said Thomas, as he continued to apply papier-mâché to the walls of the large warehouse.

"I understand your reservations, Thomas," said Mr. Willet. "But, you have to understand that to create the proper mood is going to take more than just some gels on the lighting. To be perfectly honest, the lighting in here is atrocious."

"That is true, sir," said Thomas.

"A set, when viewed closely, may not seem impressive. It may even, to some, appear sloppy," said Mr. Willet. "But, once it is seen from the audience, it will look completely different. With the correct lighting, a set can transform an entire production, becoming a character itself."

"Oh," said Thomas.

"Once we have the papier-mâché covering all

of this," said Mr. Willet, as he glared at the cold corrugated metal walls of the warehouse, "our lair will slowly come together."

"Oh," said Thomas.

Thomas turned and saw that Mr. Willet was standing in a skin-tight purple unitard. He had drawn yellow and orange lightning bolts across the arm and the legs.

"Is that what you're planning on wearing?" said Thomas.

"Well, it isn't finished," said Mr. Willet. "I mean, you aren't seeing it with the mask. And remember, the lighting in here is completely wrong."

"I didn't mean to sound judgmental," said Thomas. "I was just thinking that maybe, if you don't mind, I might make a few adjustments to it."

"Like?" said Mr. Willet.

"Well, for starters, I was thinking how nice it might be for you to have pockets."

"Really?" Said Mr. willet.

"Just as a thought," said Thomas. "I don't know what you're planning on, but they might be useful."

"Anything else?" said Mr. Willet.

"Maybe replace some of the drawn lightning bolts with some fabric, just to make it look a bit more put together," said Thomas.

"Fine," said Mr. Willet, as he began to remove the unitard.

"I hope I didn't hurt your feelings," said Thomas. "I'm certain it will be fine."

"No you don't," said Mr. Willet, as he finished removing the unitard. "Thomas, we're going to be doing some amazing comedy here. And a good deal of comedy is risk, and when you take that risk you have to be available to listen, especially if it all fails. I don't want you to ever feel like you can't speak your mind. If you think something looks bad, or are confused as to why I am doing something, I need you to speak up."

"Thank you, Mr. Willet," said Thomas.

"You are welcome, Thomas. I am looking forward to see what we accomplish."

Chapter Eighteen

Wherein Nicolas and Christina visit a gated community.

"Porn?" said Nicolas, sitting in the passenger seat of Christina's SUV.

She pulled off the 101 and onto Ventura Blvd.

"More like soft porn," said Christina. "Like a horror flick full of unnecessary boobs and sex."

"Okay," said Nicolas. "Soft porn then. That really makes all of the difference in the world now doesn't it."

"Of course it fucking matters!" said Christina. "Porn is something that is shot on the cheap and shoved up on the internet. The commercial viability of producing porn is gone. The real cash flow is creating a seemingly safe portal, a website, to get the content to the guy masturbating in front of his computer. Horror films with tits make a fuckload of money. Now that we've met with Mr. Morgan, things will start to open up."

"Open up?" said Nicolas.

"Now that you've seen him, everyone is going to want to at least meet with you," said Christina. "So, that means from here on out we can be a good deal more selective with who we take meetings with."

"So, no more porn?" said Nicolas. "No more having to check to make certain that the seat isn't sticky before I sit down?"

"Soft porn horror," said Christina. "No penetration, nothing naked from the waist down, therefore no fluids on the seat."

"Regardless, the guy was an asshole," said Nicolas.

"I can't promise you that everyone we meet is going to be respectful of your novel, or you," said Christina. "There are a lot of very desperate people out here, all of them with a brilliant idea, great story, or something else that allegedly sets them apart. If people like Mr. Morgan didn't shield themselves from the pile of shit that would be set at their feet all day everyday, it would eat them alive. Having to listen to desperate plea after desperate plea, and wanting to say yes, but knowing that there is no financial reward to green lighting a turd. They aren't trying to be assholes. After a while you have to distance yourself from it, otherwise you die a little every time you have to say no to someone, because they feel you're squashing their dreams, their very existence. And you know they're right. But, if there is no marketable aspect to it, why bother?"

"That is possibly the saddest thing I have ever heard. Why would anyone want to enter a world that doesn't surprise you any more? A world where everything is just reduced to its marketability, never seeing the amazing beauty that can be the mundane. This must be why people build such opulent homes out here. They're trying to find something to give them a fleeting sense of artistic joy."

"Do you mean to shit on everything, or is it just a gift?" said Christina.

"I just think it's sad, not being surprised by the world anymore, don't you?"

"Just relax," said Christina. "I'm not saying I don't see how fucking weird a lot of this can be, but this is just the way business is done out here. That being said, you have to remember that none of this is personal, it's just fucking business."

The SUV pulled up on a windy road that led up into the hills and ended at a large gate. As the SUV approached, the gate slowly opened. A security guard was waiting just beyond it. He waved the SUV to pull up slowly and stop. A second guard appeared at the driver's window.

"Hello," said Christina, to the guard.

"May I help you folks?" said the guard.

"We are here to see Ms. Sette," said Christina. "I believe we have an appointment."

"Yes, you do," said the guard. A man appeared in a golf cart next to them. "You will follow Ernest there in the cart."

"Sure," said Christina.

Ernest pulled in front of them in his golf cart and began slowly up the hill and turned to the left. Both sides of the narrow street were strangled by large green hedges. There were no street signs, and no way to actually mark where you were. All of the hedges matched each other. There was nothing to see out the windows other than large green walls.

"This is like a maze," said Nicolas, as they turned off the main narrow twisty path and onto another one which quickly changed from being paved asphalt to cobblestone.

"It almost feels like they're trying too hard doesn't it?" said Christina.

"I know what you mean, it is almost like, why spend all this money to seclude yourself in something that feels like a small town dropped in a hedge maze. Why not just move to he middle of no where and start planting?" said Nicolas. "Wait. Why is it okay to make fun of her and not the pornographer?"

"She's just an actress," said Christina.

The golf cart turned another corner and came to a large gate in front of what Nicolas could only imagine was the beginning of another street.

"I'll wait here," said Ernest, "to assist you on your egress from the community."

"Thank you?" said Christina, as the large gate opened before them. She allowed the car to begin to roll forward onto the driveway. She tried to not hit the line of weeping willows and magnolia tress that lined the drive up to the large house.

"It looks like a fucking plantation," said Nicolas.

"It looks like a set," said Christina.

"You've never been here?" said Nicolas.

"I set all of this up with her personal assistant," said Christina.

"What type of a person builds a fucking plantation in the middle of Los Angels?" said Nicolas.

"She does," said Christina, as she pointed to an elderly woman who was wearing in a long white dress. She was standing out front of her estate surrounded by what Nicolas assumed were people who worked in the house. They were all African-American, and dressed as traditional antebellum servants.

"What the fuck?" said Nicolas.

"That is Ms. Ellie Sette, former b-movie actress, and matriarch of one of the largest independent non-porn media empires on the West Coast."

Christina pulled the car up to the front of the house and stopped. Immediately the doors to the SUV were opened, and Nicolas and Christina were pulled from the car. A man in a red valet jacket drove the car around behind the home.

"Welcome, welcome!" said Ms. Sette, in a heavily affected drawl. Her smile was wide and blinding white. "You must be Nicolas," she continued, as she took his arm. "I have to warn you I have a soft spot for writers, especially novelists. Three of my past five husbands were writers."

"Oh," said Nicolas, as he quickly blushed.

"Isn't that sweet, he blushes!" she said. "Why don't you two follow me into the parlor and we can have a drink and discuss your amazing novella?"

The interior of the home was even more affected than the exterior. The dark hardwood paneling, the fake gas lights, large fireplaces, and velvet chairs were out of place, especially when he heard the air conditioning cycle on.

"Please make yourself comfortable," said Ms. Sette. "I'll be right back with some refreshments."

A pair of young men waited at the door, at stiff attention.

Nicolas inspected the bookshelves. They were filled with leather-bound tomes, purchased, no doubt, for their appearance rather than their content. There was a feeling of revulsion that came over him, as he spotted an old medical manual sitting next to a Victor Hugo novel, which was leaning against a book in Russian. Their placement was artistically color coordinated, but made no logical sense. This was not the manic hoarding of a bibliophile. Books placed on the floor in precarious stacks, which he or she would eventually get to once they read everything else on one of the other numerable stacks and shelves crowded with treasures and remarkable finds. These were set dressings. Nicolas wondered if the fireplace was even real.

Nicolas turned to the one of the men standing at the door.

"Ummmm," said Nicolas.

"It's all good, sir," said the first man.

"We totally understand," said the second. "It can be kind of off-putting at first."

"The woman has more money than sense," said the first. "She pays us a ridiculous amount of money to play a part."

"Just keep repeating to yourself," said the second, "it's just a part."

Ms. Sette returned with a man who was carrying a tray. On it were bottles of varying sizes, a pitcher of mint juleps, and a second pitcher of iced tea.

"Help yourself to whatever you like," she said

with a broad smile. "I'll check with Mamie in the kitchen. She was working on finger sandwiches."

"Are you fucking kidding me?" said Nicolas.

"I understand that this is very culturally insensitive," said Christina. "But, you were saying you get paid a large sum of money. How large are we talking?"

"What the hell does that matter?" said Nicolas. "These people are selling their dignity."

"And how is that any different from you?" said the man with the tray of drinks.

"Mamie said the sandwiches are going to take a bit longer," said Ms. Sette, as she returned to the room and sank into the velvet couch. She signaled to one of the men at the door and he placed a record on an antique phonograph. "I hope you don't mind, but I have recently become obsessed with Bach's violin concertos. I love listening to the minor embellishments from different recordings. I find it amazing how musicians and conductors when faced with the same piece of music, can make it their own with the simplest of trills, or slight pause before a kick of extra emphasis on a specific note. Don't you?"

"I do enjoy music," said Nicolas, as he helped

himself to a glass of iced tea. "But, I have always been that person who finds one copy of a song enough. I don't need to amass covers, nor do I feel the need to find the first recording of the original artist. I usually find a version that I enjoy and stick with that."

"I like a man who knows what he wants," said Ms. Sette.

"No, I'm just usually too broke to afford to buy multiple copies of much of anything," said Nicolas.

"Of course, the starving artist!" said Ms. Sette. "Shall we see what we can do about that?"

"It is a beautiful home you have here Ms. Sette," said Christina.

"Thank you," she said curtly, before turning back to Nicolas. "Your book, I have to say moved me deeply."

"Wow," said Nicolas. "Thank you."

"However, I do have a few questions regarding the book," said Ms. Sette.

"Like what?" said Christina.

"Well, really it's a few question and requests," said Ms. Sette.

"Go right ahead," said Nicolas.

"First, the title. How married are you to it?"

"Why does no one like the title?" said Nicolas.

"I'm just thinking that there may be something else that we might be able to find to really grab the audience," said Ms. Sette. "What about, 'Black Snow'?"

"I love it," said Nicolas. "As the title for a brilliant Russian novel that no one west of the Rockies has read."

"I see," she said. "How historically accurate is it?"

"To be honest not too terribly," said Nicolas. "It takes place roughly during the Battle of the Bulge, the final months of World War Two. I do play a good deal with the locations, as well as the time of year, making it a bit snowier and colder than it actually would have been."

"I see," she said. "That being said how necessary would you say the Nazis are?"

"What?" said Nicolas.

"I understand how difficult this may be," said Ms. Sette. "I urge you, please don't get defensive, and keep an open mind. Do we really need the Nazis?"

"Instead of just regular German soldiers?"

said Nicolas. "I guess that would be alright, but I think some of the flashbacks need the level of savagery and stereotypical knee jerk reaction most people have to the goose step and the swastika."

"And there you've hit on it," she said, "the stereotyping of the Germans as all being evil."

"That's why I made the female lead German," said Nicolas.

"She is?" she said.

"She is the daughter of a Lutheran minister," he said.

"Is that actually mentioned in the book?"

"Anton finds her in the church," he said. "There is a whole chapter where they do nothing but discuss faith. The one where they find the man crucified in the woods."

"Must have missed that as well," she said.

"Did you actually read the book?" said Nicolas.

"Me, personally?" she said. "No, but, I did have my assistant write up a glowing summary. I'll have to have a word with her about her omissions. It even said that the book didn't have an actual ending. There seems to be a bit of a disconnect here, and for that I apologize. I have lined up a few potential backers, but one of them is a large Bavarian conglomerate. They are kind of sensitive about all these issues, if you know what I mean."

"The book does have an ending," said Nicolas.

"Sorry," intervened Christina. "Nick here is feeling a bit defensive. Nothing to do with you, just more general frustration. I think what you may be asking is could we take the Germans out of it all together, and still be able to live with it?"

"Actually, even more than that," she said. "I was thinking why not set it in the distant future? Out among the stars?"

"So, you want to take my book about a concentration camp escapee during the final days of World War Two, remove any mention of the Germans, as well as place it in the distant future, not during any war?

"That was my thought," she said. "If it worked with Shakespeare and 'The Tempest', why not with this? Did you ever see 'Forbidden Planet'? And we would have to do something about the title. Have you considered 'Black Snow'?"

"For a futuristic film set in space?" said Nicolas. "Why would you even bother optioning the book if you aren't going to use it?"

"Because, it's the one that everyone is talking about," said Ms. Sette.

"I think now might be a good time to leave," said Nicolas.

"Why would you say that?" said Christina. "Why don't we finish hearing what the woman has to say?"

"You did," she said.

"Well, you've given us an awful lot to think about," said Christina. "Thank you so much. And I am very sorry for his brashness."

"No," she said. "There is no need to apologize for him. He sees what is on the page as art. I view it as a commodity. That was why I had my assistant read it. If I had, I am certain that I might get lost in it, that somewhere in the narrative there may be a moment so beautiful that I wouldn't be able to make an objective proposal."

"I thank you for understanding," said Christina. "I am certain that once I have a moment to talk to him-"

"And I'm certain you've got other meetings to get to," she said.

"Thank you," said Christina, as she followed Nicolas out of the house. Their SUV was waiting for them.

Christina nodded to everyone as she got into the drivers seat. Nicolas sulked into passenger seat.

"What the fuck was that?" said Christina, as she pulled down the long driveway.

"I don't know, she was completely self-obsessed and condescending," said Nicolas.

"I'm not talking about her, I'm talking about you," said Christina. "What the fuck is wrong with you?"

"She wanted to take the Germans out of the war and make it into some kind of sci-fi bullshit!" said Nicolas. "It would have been completely unrecognizable from my book."

"Fine," said Christina, "for Christmas I'll send her a fucking history book."

Chapter Nineteen

Wherein Mr. Willet hatches a diabolical joke.

Thomas stood in the middle of the warehouse and admired his work. He thought it was amazing how right Mr. Willet had been. It looked great. The rock forms were amazing and gave the space the feel that it was deep in a cave hidden away from the rest of the world. There was an ornate chair, which looked like a throne that looked down onto four television monitors.

Thomas had been adjusting the light levels and changing gels for most of the day. He knew that Mr. Willet would be pleased.

Mr. Willet walked in from the bathroom that was behind the large rock formation, wearing the new unitard, which Thomas had made for him. The lighting bolts were sharp and really popped against the dark blue background.

"What do you think?" said Mr. Willet.

Thomas took a deep breath summoned all of

his courage and very meekly said, "For the third time, I don't know how it is going to look until you put on the goggles, sir. Sorry, sir."

"No, there is nothing for you to apologize for. Looking here at all of the fine work you've done, I must congratulate you, it looks magnificent."

"I have to thank you for that, sir. If it wasn't for your guidance I don't think I would have been able to actually stick with it to get the job done. Without your vision I doubt I would have been able to see what could be accomplished here."

"I think that you give me too much credit," said Mr. Willet. "Regardless, I know that no matter what happens here that the hard wok which we are busy pursuing, will continue; that all of this will help with the punch line, even if something were to happen to me."

"Please don't say that, sir."

"No," said Mr. Willet, as he ascended the rock formation and stood in front of the monitors. "It is a definite possibility. I may not return. I very well may not make it to the punch line. This is why we have partners in comedy. So, that one of us can work on the set-up while the other delivers the punch line."

Mr. Willet pulled the hood of the costume up and over his hairline. Then he placed the brass goggles over his eyes. Looking like a villain straight out of an 80's comic book, he struck a pose before continuing, "You, my friend, may have to deliver the punch line someday."

"But," said Thomas, "I'm not ready."

"I know," said Mr. Willet. "But, when the time comes I hope you are."

"I hope I am as well," said Thomas.

"Look, not that I expect anything to actually happen to me," said Mr. Willet. "But, if anything does I want you to open this envelope."

He pulled a large manila envelope out of a pocket, and tossed it down to Thomas.

"But, be certain not to open it unless something happens to me," said Mr. Willet.

"That sounds terribly cryptic, and to be perfectly honest kind of scary," said Thomas.

"No, Thomas, my good man, there is no reason to be frightened. Now is the time for us to rejoice! Now is the time to repent! Now is the time for the greatest joke of all time!"

Chapter Twenty

Wherein Nicolas and Christina take the stairs.

Christina and Nicolas sat in the SUV outside of the office building on Wilshire Boulevard. The two office towers were ultra modern when they had been built forty years ago. Now they just looked like large grey monoliths in the midst of a neighborhood that had in the past thirty-seven years seen urban blight, and now was experiencing an ironic gentrification. Old bars, which had once specialized in the cashing of social security checks, now hosted hipsters making cocktails using artisanal bitters, while cashing the regulars' unemployment checks.

Christina and Nicolas walked past the sleeping security guard and to a large bank of elevators, three of which were out of order. Nicolas looked at the beige tile, and imagined the thousands of suits that passed through this lobby, thinking about how they felt about the world they inhabited in all of its modern glory. The building screamed the end off the boom that was the mid-seventies. Blind to its own faults, it couldn't foresee the recession, the gas rationing, the riots, O.J., the rise and decline and rebranding of Los Angeles. It was just there in all of its seventies beige glory.

Christina pushed the button for the seventeenth floor. The door closed, and then re-opened. Christina pushed the button again, and the door just opened and closed.

Nicolas reached over and pressed the buttons for the sixteenth, seventeenth and eighteenth floors. A loud bell rang, the doors closed, and the elevator car lurched to the left slightly before it began to slowly ascend to the sixteenth floor. The grinding of the gears and the equipment could be heard loudly from the inside of the elevator car.

"I want to make conversation," said Nicolas. "But, I'm afraid if I talk too loud that I may kill us all."

Christina began to giggle.

"Don't laugh," said Nicolas, as he began to. "The vibrations!"

A few minutes later the doors creaked open on the sixteenth floor. Laughing, Christina and Nicolas threw themselves out of the elevator. Out of the corner of his eye Nicolas thought he saw a man in a black unitard with yellow lightning bolts on it duck into an office. They quickly made it to the fire stairs.

"You can't smoke here," said the woman in the stairwell. She had been standing behind the door.

"Thank you," said Christina, as she started to walk up to the seventeenth floor.

"You can't smoke up their either, it is against the law to smoke here!" said the woman.

"We understand, we don't smoke," said Nicolas.

"Really?" she said.

"I had no idea that it was illegal to smoke in a stairwell," said Christina.

"See!" she said. "I fucking knew it."

"You fucking knew what?" said Christina.

"That you were coming in here to smoke," said the woman. She adjusted her dress and smoothed the hair on the side of her head that was pulled back into a tight bun.

"No," said Nicolas. "Neither of us smoke."

"But, you just said!"

"No, ma'am," said Nicolas. "We admitted that we had no idea that it was illegal to smoke in a stairwell. That doesn't mean that we were going to smoke in the stairwell."

"No, now you're just denying it, because you're caught," she said.

"Who the fuck are you?" said Christina.

"I'm the person who caught you trying to smoke in the stairwell," she said.

"Yeah, but why?" said Christina. "Why the hell would you want to be that person? Wouldn't a sign do the trick? Something simple, like 'No Fucking Smoking!' have you tried that?"

"It didn't work," she said.

"Why does it matter?" said Nicolas.

"Because, you're not supposed to do it!"

"We weren't going to!" said Nicolas.

"I'm going to have to report you," she said.

"To who?" said Christina.

"To whom," corrected Nicolas.

"Fuck off," admonished Christina.

"Look, just give me your names, and I'm going to report you to the building management."

"No," said Christina.

"What?" she said. "I demand that you tell me your names."

"No," said Christina, as she began to continue up the stairs.

Nicolas followed her.

"This isn't over," she called after them.

"No, I really think it might be," said Nicolas, as he followed Christina through the fire door to the seventeenth floor.

"So, our options for escape right now, are an old elevator, or dealing with the tattletale in the stairwell," said Nicolas, as the walked down the corridor looking for the office.

"This is beginning to have the feel of a disaster movie isn't it?" said Christina, as she opened the door to an office.

The building belied the office inside. There were spotless glass windows behind spotless glass doors, which housed beautiful people who were sitting on minimalist Scandinavian furniture. The simple lines and wood grain of the furniture were mirrored on the walls.

"Hello," said the receptionist. "How may I assist you?"

"We're here to see Tyler," said Christina.

"Who?" said the receptionist.

"Tyler," said Christina. "I'm sorry, I have to admit that I didn't realize that you've redone the office like this."

"May I ask what your appointment is involving?" said the receptionist.

"It has something to do with my book," said Nicolas.

"And which book would that be," she said condescendingly.

"It's called, Crazy Rhythm," said Nicolas.

"Oh, my God!" she said, as her face lit up. "You don't understand how much I loved that book! I'm certain that Marvin will want to meet with you ASAP. May I get you a cup of coffee or some mineral water?"

"I'd love a water," said Nicolas.

"Sparkling or still?"

"Sparkling, please," said Nicolas.

Before Christina could answer, she disappeared into the mirrored enclosure behind her.

"Who is Marvin?" said Nicolas.

"I'll be honest, I think I may have fucked up a

bit," said Christina. "I think we might be in the wrong office. There is every possibility that I made a mistake with the address. I'm going to make a quick phone call. Wait here."

Christina pulled out her cell phone and desperately searched for a signal. She exited the office and began walking back toward the fire stairs.

Nicolas alone in the lobby, felt accomplished for a moment. He felt that this was the Hollywood experience that he had been waiting for. He didn't feel icky in here. A man who was very tan walked out from behind the glass doors, followed by the receptionist who was holding a bottle of sparkling mineral water for Nicolas. Not a single hair on his head looked even remotely out of place. His teeth were bleached white, and not the cheap blue white one gets from strips you buy at the drug store. No, this was a proper dentist whitening. He wore a blue suit that fit him perfectly.

Flashing his smile he said, "Hello, Nicolas. I'm Marvin, and I think through an entertaining series of missteps, you have arrived at my office. Let's talk about your book."

"But, my friend, Christina," said Nicolas.

"Let me guess, she's been acting as your agent," said Marvin. "Don't stress it, she'll get her ten percent. But, I would much rather talk with you about your amazing book. Is that okay?"

Marvin and the receptionist quickly led him back to an expansive office. Marvin motioned for Nicolas to make himself comfortable on the leather couch. Nicolas took a seat and looked out the window. Los Angeles unfolded in front of him, leading all the way to the Hollywood Hills. Just to the right of the Hollywood sign, a small trail of black smoke rose up and was swept away by the Santa Ana winds.

"Nice office," said Nicolas.

"An amazing piece of literature," said Marvin. "And its explosive popularity is something to take advantage of right now. I'm going to put my cards on the table, and without anyone else here to muck it up, I hope you'll just be honest with me as well."

"I'll try, Marvin," said Nicolas, as he was handed his bottle of mineral water, and the receptionist took a seat next to him. Nicolas hadn't noticed how attractive she was until she sat next to him and smiled.

"This is one of those things that if we can put it together quickly, you will be a very wealthy man," said Marvin. "And your next novel will be a guaranteed best seller. Doesn't matter if it's shit or not, all it will have to say is, 'The next novel from the author of Crazy Rhythm,' and it will fly off the shelves. But, if we wait this is going to live in development hell for a very long time, which will realistically be neither here nor there for you. You're going to get paid for the rights to offer it up for development, whether it gets made or not. But, it matters to me, because if I don't make this movie, I don't get paid.

"Now if it does get made, and quickly, you'll get both that paycheck as well as another substantial one for your percentage of the film, as well as however much you make from your next book, which, as I said, will clearly be a bestseller.

"I'm certain that you have a good deal of meetings to take, but here I think we're the only one's big enough to actually put together the right deal. I'm not going to rush it. I'm not talking some bullshit b-movie horror flick that a few college roommates make in a couple of weeks. I'm talking an eighteen-month adventure that starts as soon as you sign a few documents. Then I give you a check for a quarter of a million dollars, minus your friend's ten percent. Eighteen months later we're premiering Crazy Rhythm. What do you say?"

"What do you need from me?" said Nicolas.

"Nothing," said Marvin. "All I need is a few signatures, and then you head back to Chicago, get cracking on your next novel. We'll take care of everything here."

"What if I want Christina to be involved?" said Nicolas.

"Sure she can," said Marvin. "We'll make certain that you both get Executive Producer credits. What do you say?"

Christina walked back into the office followed by the woman from the stairwell.

"I don't see how the hell it is you can deny it now," she said.

"For the sixth fucking time I was only searching for enough bars to make a goddamnend phone call!" said Christina. "What is your fucking problem?"

"I don't like it when people break the rules! Do you understand that?"

"Fine, as soon as I fucking break one I will be certain to inform you, so that you may upbraid me accordingly," said Christina. "Wait!"

"What?"

"Wait!" said Christina. "Shut up!"

"Why?"

"Because, I fucking asked nicely," said Christina. "Where is Nicolas?"

"Who?" said the woman, "The other smoker? I've got you! I know who the hell you are. Now that I know one of your names, you are in so much trouble!" The woman stormed out of the office.

Christina looked around manically looking for the receptionist, and suddenly caught a glimpse of Nicolas on the other side of the glass, smiling and shaking hands. The door opened and Nicolas, Marvin and the receptionist emerged.

"And this must be, Christina," said Marvin. "Well, I would like to say that by staying out of the way you have earned your ten percent."

"I told you to stay put," said Christina, as they walked back to the SUV.

"What am I, a dog?" said Nicolas. "I don't understand what your problem is! For the next few days we can just relax and enjoy ourselves.

"I just spent the past fifteen minutes groveling to get you another appointment with someone, in the hope that they might just be able to fit you in," said Christina, "while arguing with crazy stair lady."

"I really don't understand what it is you're trying to accomplish," said Nicolas. "Were we supposed to put together a deal? If that was the case, we have one. Let's say it was a success and head home."

"You don't get it, do you?" she said, as she climbed behind the wheel of the SUV. Nicolas sat in the passenger seat, and before he had a chance to shut the door, Christina sped out into traffic.

"Dude, what is wrong?" said Nicolas.

"I gave my word that I would have you at this meeting, half an hour ago," said Christina. "Now I have to get you up to Sunset in fifteen minutes to meet with Tyler and Saul."

"But, why does it matter?" said Nicolas. "We've signed a deal, hell I even got you an Executive Producer credit. Why don't we just head home, or to a hotel, or for a drink? You look like you could use a drink."

"This is more important that a deal," said Christina. "This is my reputation."

"Don't stress it," said Nicolas.

"Don't stress it?" said Christina. "Fuck you! You haven't heard a fucking thing I've said to you all fucking day! You get to be the aloof artist here. You haven't stopped judging me, or everyone around you since you got off that fucking plane, turning your nose up at people who are in the industry, who have put together a fuck-load more movies than either of us! Sure you're the artist, which is a full rung higher than the talent. If you were an actor or a screen writer or any other type of commodity that regularly trolls these streets desperately looking for a fucking gig, then you would be out on your ass with an attitude like this. Shit, you don't even have a fucking clue how hard this is. If you were this much of an asshole, no one would work with you. You would be barred from even taking a fucking meeting. But, you've done something they can't do, something that happens once in a lifetime. You've captured lighting in a bottle! Just by being in the right place at the right time! You got lucky! You're a fucking step up from an internet meme! And the only reason you're a step up is because they know how to make fucking green off your sorry ass.

"Where the fuck do you get the balls to look down on us? Fuck you! I have to deal with these people when you're gone. These are my co-workers, these are my cubicle buddies. These are the people who get shit done, and I had a chance to finally get to seat at the grown up table, and you took it away from me! ASSHOLE!"

They rode in silence, past the Tar Pits, and up toward the hills. Turing onto sunset, they pulled up in front of a modest sized building.

"I'm sorry," said Nicolas, as a man in a unitard with lightning bolts on it dove behind some bushes on the other side of the street. "Um, did you see that?"

"What?" said Christina.

"That guy dive behind the bushes over there?" said Nicolas.

"They're probably rehearsing," said Christina. "You see some strange shit around here. And it's okay. I know you didn't mean to fuck me, that you're just an ignorant dip shit."

"Thank you?" said Nicolas. "What do you need me to do in there?"

"Honestly, just stand there and look like you've written a best seller that they want to buy," said Christina, "and, please don't mention the deal."

"You've got it," said Nicolas.

The office was small and cramped. The building had a certain retro charm, which quickly put Nicolas in mind of a claustrophobic film noir movie.

"Look," said Saul, "I've gotten you two five minutes, please don't let it be a waste of time."

"We'll try," said Nicolas.

Tyler was an affable guy, rosy cheeks and a white smile. A small window behind him looked out onto the Hollywood Hills. Nicolas spotted the same small plume of black smoke coming up out of them.

Nicolas was about to comment on the plume of smoke when the first shot rang out. It wasn't that unusual to hear a gun shot for any of them. But, there is always that moment when most people who have never been to a war zone, where they wonder if they heard what they thought they heard.

Saul, Nicolas, Tyler and Christina all did the same thing, they were about to ask if what they had just heard was in fact a gun shot, when, as if to confirm their suspicions, another shot rang out. It sounded closer than the last.

Tyler edged his way toward a closet, Saul and Christina ducked behind Tyler's desk, and Nicolas stood staring out at the black smoke that rose from the hills.

Once the man in the unitard broke in, there was nowhere to hide. There was no way to pretend that Nicolas didn't see him. How do you pretend to not see a forty-year-old man in a unitard with lightning bolts and brass goggles?

Tyler slammed the closet door shut behind him.

Nicolas thought about turning around and looking back at the small picture window. If he just took a moment to look at the smoke in the Hollywood Hills, maybe someone would jump out and admit that this was a joke, or a nightmare. He could just wake up back in his crappy apartment in Chicago. Nicolas looked down at the gun the man was holding and swallowed hard.

"Umm, the craftsmanship on your outfit is really very remarkable," said Nicolas.

"Thank you, very much," said the man in the

unitard. Nicolas thought his voice sounded familiar.

"Nick," said Christina, from behind the desk. "Get down."

"Why?" said Nicolas. "It's not like the office is really that huge, where the fuck could I go? I'm pretty sure he could shoot me just as easily standing as kneeling."

"Are you trying to be some kind of a hero?" said Christina.

"No, I'm just to scared to move."

"Have you pissed yourself?"

"Not yet," said Nicolas.

"I think it would be a really good idea, if I left," said Tyler, from behind the closet door. "I think that if I were to remove myself from this situation, it might end up diffusing a good deal of the tension here."

"Really?" said Nicolas. "I think that maybe asking the guy with the gun to leave might do more to diffuse the situation."

"I think he might actually be wanting to point the gun at me," continued the muffled voice from the closet.

"Is that so?" said Nicolas. "Why would he

rather be pointing the gun at you, Tyler?"

"Nick, call me Ty," said the closet.

"Please don't call me Nick." Nicolas turned to the man in the spandex.

"It makes me really very happy that you prefer to be called Nicolas," said the man in the spandex. "Nicolas has gravitas, Nick is belittling. He is correct though, I would rather be pointing the gun at Ty."

As he said this he slowly began raising the gun, away from Nicolas' chest and taking aim at the closet behind him. Unfortunately, as it reached Nicolas' head the gun fired. This was completely unintentional, and if the man in the spandex had been informed of the gun's hair trigger, he never would have purchased it. However, sensing that everything was quickly going from bad to worse, he turned and ran out of the office, shortly before Nicolas' body hit the floor.

Chapter Twenty-One

The third excerpt from <u>Crazy Rhythm</u> by Nicolas Irons

Anton walked around the side of the large church. Behind it he saw a large hill, which led up to an inviting tree. On a summer day he could imagine the children running up and down the hill, laughing and releasing the joyful sounds their parents had forced them to silence during a lengthy Sunday service. Anton smiled, he loved the idea of children dismissing the theological lessons of the homily and just enjoying a hill. The large boots Anton was wearing caught on a toolbox, tipping it over. Its contents spilled over the cobblestones and landed next to a dead priest in his full vestments. Anton thought about saying a few words, but couldn't remember what they should be. The body lay across a small red door, which led into the church. The body was much heavier than Anton had expected. The other bodies that Anton had encountered had all been emaciated, and picked over by other scavengers, little left but skin and bones. This body was fresh. The priest had probably only died a day or two ago. Anton had to grunt and struggle to shift the body, so he could access the door.

The red door creaked open. It sounded like something out of an old movie. Inside many of the pews had been overturned and were now being used for firewood in the center of the church. Anton kept to the far walls and tried not to make much noise. The shadows given off by the dancing flames made it easy for Anton to find places to hide.

Next to the fire a small bundle of rags moved. Anton slowly moved towards it. A small cough could be heard. Poking out through the rags was a small face. Anton smiled at the young boy who was bundled up next to the fire. His head was dripping with sweat. He opened his eyes and recoiled at the image of Anton.

Then looking at his coat he said simply, "American."

"What?" said Anton. "Me? No, I just found this."

"American," said the boy again.

"What's wrong?" said Anton. "Can't you understand me?"

"Guttentag?" called out the voice of young woman. "Vas is das? Hallo? Spreken sie Deutch?"

Anton's instinct was to run, every fiber of him screamed, "RUN! NOW! RUN!" But, the fire was warm. He couldn't remember the last time he had felt warm.

Anton looked up to see who had called to him. Anton figured she was probably sixteen. Her dirty auburn hair was pulled back tightly. Her face was cute, with few freckles and more dirt and ash than she knew. She had a cane that she used to help her walk toward the fire. It was obvious to Anton that the young girl was blind.

"Eine klien Deutch," said Anton. He looked at her nose, how it came to a cute bulbous point at the end.

"American," said the boy.

"Then you speak English?"

"Yes," said Anton. "I do."

"So, tell me," said the girl. "Have you come to liberate us, or steal our food?"

"I haven't decided yet," said Anton. "But, I

have some chocolate, if you would care for some."

They young boy said something quickly to the girl in German. The girl said something back.

"What is your name?" said the girl.

"Anton," he said.

"That doesn't sound very American," she said.

"Well, what is your name?"

"Abigail," she said.

"That doesn't sound very German," said Anton. "And what about your brother here?"

"His name is Hans," said Abigail.

"I had an Uncle Hans," said Anton. "Hans would you care for some chocolate?" Before the young boy could answer, Anton pulled a chocolate bar from his gun holster and handed it to the boy. He quickly whispered something to his sister.

"He wants to know why you have chocolate in your holster?" she said.

"Easier to digest than a gun," he said. "I know you don't know me, but would it be okay if I were to spend the night here, with you?"

"I don't know, without my father here," said Abigail. "He left to find supplies to secure the door."

Before she could finish, Anton was already

slipping into a deep sleep.

Uncle Hans stood in the middle of the grey mud with the marionette. Anton wondered if the soil, or the ash that kept falling from the sky was to blame for the increasingly grey pallor to the world. He knew that Hans' color was due to a lack of food, as was with most of the people at the camp. The soldiers were standing and laughing at Uncle with his marionette, except for one soldier with a red armband. He stood there scowling in disapproval. He grabbed the marionette from Uncle. Uncle lunged at the marionette, and was hit. He landed hard. The officer with the red armband kicked him hard in the side. Instinctually, Anton rose to try to get them to stop. The world went black with stars again.

The rocking of the boxcar woke him. As he lay on the ground, people kept stepping on him. Uncle tried to get them to stop, but there just wasn't enough room. There was nowhere else for them to stand. The boxcar came to a hard stop. The sound of voices could be heard as the box car was uncoupled, and the side door was flown open. The bullets came quickly and Anton was pinned to the floor by the bodies of the others in the boxcar as they fell on top of him. The blood began to pool near Anton's face. He tried not to call out. A quick call for them to hurry up was met with the sound of the rest of the train tearing off. Anton tried to climb out of the pile of bodies that were on top of him. He fought with them, clawing his way up, until he could see daylight.

Becoming untangled from the covers he looked up at the smoldering ashes, and over to the small boy who was no longer sweating. His blue lips beguiled the hope that his fever had broken. Anton could tell from here that the boy was very, very dead.

"Anton," said his wife's voice. "What are we going to do?"

"It will be fine," said Anton. "I'll take care of it."

A child's convulsive cough could be heard from the other room. Anton walked across the worn carpet to the bedroom. There in the large bed, lay a small boy, Anton's son. He smiled at his father weakly.

"I'm going to go out now and find you some medicine," said Anton. "I need you to be a good boy for Mommy, okay." The boy moved to speak, but erupted into another convulsion of coughing.

Anton turned to rush out the door to find some medicine for the boy.

Anton wiped his eyes. The small boy on the floor of the church, so still, so tiny. He reached down to pull the covers back and revealed the tan uniform that the small boy was wearing, it even had the red armband. Anton stared at the small body.

"Daddy," said his son's voice. "You know what you need to do don't you Daddy?"

"I don't know if that is something I should-"

"Daddy, can I please help," said his son's voice. "I promise I won't get in the way. But, if you are going to do it you need to do it before she wakes up. Then we can have some real fun. Then we can show her what we've done, Daddy. Do you think she'll like it?"

"No, she won't like it. She won't like it at all."

Anton picked up the body and walked out the red door, stopping only to pick up the small toolbox.

He marched up the steep hill with the body, the little ball of hate in a Hitler youth uniform.

At the tree the first few nails bent. Anton knew it had more to do with him than the nails or the tree. Then the next few didn't work, because they tore through the flesh of the little boy's hands, until Anton remembered that the nails should go through the wrists; more precisely, below the wrists, if they were going to support the young boy's weight. That was the way they had it inside the church. Anton finished. He realized he was sweating.

"You did a very good job, Daddy," said his son's voice. "I can't wait until she gets to see."

"Hallo?" called Abigail. "Anton? Hans? Where are you?"

"We're here at the tree at the top of the hill," called down Anton.

"What are you doing up there?" said Abigail. "Where is Hans? Is he with you?"

"It is a surprise," said Anton. "Come and see."

Abigail began walking up the slick slope. She quickly lost her footing and fell.

"It's very cold out here," said Abigail. "I'm not certain that Hans should be out here. What are you doing?"

"You have to come and see what I've been doing with your little Fürer," said Anton.

"Please, I don't understand and I'm starting to get frightened. What are you talking about?"

"What is there to understand? The uniform your little Nazi brother was in!"

"What uniform?" said Abigail, as she reached the tree. "I found some dry clothes in a closet and I put him in them. He had caught a cold, and I just wanted to keep him dry. Now could you please explain to me what is going on."

Anton looked at the small, desecrated, crucified body of the innocent child. He tried to speak, but noting would come. In the distance the sound of a convoy of trucks could be heard coming towards them.

"On the ground now!" said Anton.

Abigail didn't hesitate, throwing herself to the ground. The caravan rolled through. Their engines echoed through the empty valley.

"Can I get up now?" said Abigail.

"I'm sorry, Daddy," said his son's voice.

"Don't worry I'm going to make this right," said Anton. A small cough could be heard.

"What is going on?" said Abigail.

"I am very sorry," said Anton, as he led her back down the hill. "My battalion just rolled through and they took your brother on ahead."

"Why did you let them take him!" said Abigail. "You should have told me!"

"There was neither room, nor time," said Anton. "We have to get him to a mobile hospital as quickly as possible."

"Will you take me to him, please?" said Abigail.

"I don't know if that would be the best of ideas," said Anton. "It isn't the best, as far as the road conditions. We would have to do it on foot."

"It's because I'm German isn't it?" said Abigail. "You think that we all wanted this war. My father was the pastor here for years, and all he ever did was preach peace, even for the Jews. We didn't fall in with that crowd, but if you keep thinking we did, then maybe I would be better off just staying here. I wouldn't want to get in your way."

"Wow, you're obstinate," said Anton. "Look, I just wanted you to realize that it isn't going to be easy, especially with you being blind."

"I don't care," said Abigail. "I need you to take me to my brother. I need to know he's safe."

Anton looked up the hill at the desecrated body of the boy.

"Fine," he said. "But, you have to understand that you aren't my responsibility. If you fall behind, then you fall behind. I've got a schedule to keep, and we need to get going. Let's pack up some food and get going." Anton began walking in the direction the convoy came from.

"Wait, I thought the trucks went the other way," said Abigail.

"They did," said Anton. "But, we need to go this way."

"Through the forest?" she said.

"Yes, it will be safer if we go this way," said Anton. "My men said the road should be clear, but not to take any chances. You see, when you take chances you shouldn't, people can get hurt, or even worse, killed. So, are you going to pack up any food, or should we just go?"

"My father is dead, isn't he," she asked.

"Yes," said Anton. "I'm very sorry."

"Don't be, I already knew," said Abigail, as tears flowed down her cheek. "I just wasn't ready to admit it."

"Come, now," said Anton. "No time for that, we need to get packed."

"There isn't anything to pack up," she said.

"Then, Let's get going," said Anton. "Hopefully, we'll find something before we settle down for the night, but if we don't I've got a little something for us."

"I guess I should say thank you," she said.

"For what?" he said.

"For saving us," she said.

"Do you need to hold onto my arm or anything, or will you be okay," he said.

"I'll be fine until we reach the forest," she said. "I grew up in this village. I know my way around."

"Have you always been blind?" said Anton.

"No," she said. "Will it be very far?"

"Yes."

"Anton," said his wife. Anton turned to see where her voice was coming from to find her running toward him, up the cobblestone street. The street lamps were on and a dull fog muffled the sound of her shoes.

"What's wrong?" said Anton, as he pulled his jacket tighter against himself.

"It is our son," she said. "He's run away."

Anton smiled at her and said, "He hasn't run away. Why would he run away?"

"I don't know, maybe something happened in school today, maybe he's frightened, or maybe he has gone off to fight the Germans. I don't know what crazy ideas he's come up with! But, he has them and you're going to have to see what you can do to get them out of his stupid head, and bring him home again. He took all of the canned kippers."

"He hates the canned kippers."

"Maybe he was in a hurry? I'm worried, Anton."

"Of course you are," said Anton. "I'll find him, you just get home and get the kettle on. In this night air he'll need something warm when we get back."

"You're dismissing me," she said.

"You're panicking," he said. "Just calm down and I'll take care of it."

"Promise you won't come back without him?"

"I promise."

Anton's wife turned and kissed him on the

cheek. She walked back to the apartment. Anton turned and walked toward the canal. He knew where his son would be, the same place he was last time.

His son was sitting on the wall next to the canal in a thin shirt and short pants.

"You're going to catch something if you keep coming out like that," said Anton.

"I know, Daddy," said his son. "I'm sorry."

"For what?" said Anton.

"For that," he said, motioning to the canal. By the edge of it were open tins and a few of the kippers floating in the canal.

"What happened?" said Anton.

"Well, I thought if they went swimming that they might taste better. My friend at school says that fresh fish tastes better than the kippers out of the can. So, I thought that if I let these fish swim a bit they would taste better, and Mommy would be happy that she didn't have to eat another can of kippers again. I don't think she likes the canned kippers."

"She doesn't," said Anton. "But, you do know that those fish are dead, and there isn't anything that you can actually do to them to make them not dead, don't you?"

"Of course I do, Daddy," said his son. "But, I have a bigger question for you. Do you know that helping her isn't going to bring me back, or Mommy, or that little boy? I know you want it to, but it can't."

"I know."

"So why are you doing it? You know you don't have to, so why are you?"

Chapter Twenty-Two

Wherein Mr. Willet argues with a billboard.

Mr. Willet walked out of the old building and into the midday sun on Sunset Boulevard. He fought the urge to run with every fiber of his being. Only guilty people run, and he wasn't guilty. What had happened was not what he had intended. The punch line was off, and sometimes in comedy that happens. Sometimes, the risk that is taken may simply cause one to fall flat on his or her face. So, much of comedy is being willing to take that risk. The only thing to do is pick yourself back up and prepare one's self for the next joke. The gun was still in his hand. He stowed it in one of his hidden pockets.

"Hey!" screamed a voice behind him. Mr. Willet had never been one to have much respect for authority figures. He didn't have the knee jerk reaction that most people have when someone yells out for attention. He was not going to be distracted by what may be his last performance. He had dealt with hecklers before. He never much enjoyed doing stand up, the form itself was just so limiting. The entire joke/punch line dynamic was dated, and there was really very little to be mined out of it. But, sketches like this were something completely different.

The sound of sirens came blaring up from behind him. Mr. Willet ignored it as he continued to walk along Sunset Boulevard. People began to crowd the street, as the line of police cars rolled up along side Mr. Willet, cell phones were removed from pockets, purses, and man bags. All were pointed at the scene, hoping to capture the rantings of a madman and/or police brutality.

"Sir!" screamed one of the officers, as he pointed his gun at Mr. Willet. "I'm going to have to ask you to freeze! Get your ass down, or I will shoot it! Do you understand me?"

"Wait," screamed another of the officers, "do you have any idea who that man is?"

"A dumb mother fucker who is about to be shot!" said the first officer.

"Dude, that is Mr. Willet," said the second.

"The self-proclaimed king of late night."

"He would be a fucking celebrity, wouldn't he?" said the first officer as he holstered his weapon. "Fuck!"

Mr. Willet smiled, as he heard them scream expletives. In the distance there was the distinct noise that heralded the imminent arrival of the major news outlets. Now was his chance, he thought, as the police cruisers, mob of bystanders armed with their cell phones, and news choppers began to slowly follow behind him. He felt like he was at the head of a parade leading them to understand precisely what it was that was happening. He could find the fucking billboard, and then they would all understand. He could save the joke! He wasn't crazy, just driven over the edge by poor grammar.

The parade wound down Sunset, until it reached a bend in the road. There above the old record store was one of the offending billboards. Mr. Willet turned back to the parade and smiled.

"See?" said Mr. Willet.

"See what?" said the officer. He pulled his car to a stop in front of Mr. Willet. The rest of the police cars, and bystanders filled in behind him.

The news choppers hovering made it difficult to hear what he was saying.

"The sign," said Mr. Willet. "The fucking billboard!"

"What about it?" said the officer. "Do you not like the gym? Who does? That's no reason to go shooting people."

"I didn't mean to shoot him," said Mr. Willet. "It was all just a joke."

"Then why did you run?" said the officer.

"Look at how I'm dressed!" said Mr. Willet. "Do you think anyone would listen to me? Here is the point to all of this. Look at the billboard. Don't just look at what it's saying! Look at how it's saying it!"

The officer looked at the toned woman in he billboard and the large letters that went across her torso reading, "TEST YOU'RE METAL".

"Was the billboard talking to, sir?" said the officer. "If the billboard was talking there is someone who can help that."

"No, the fucking words on the billboard, jackass! Read the words."

"What about it, sir?" said the officer. "Someone used the incorrect your, but that's become part of the marketing. Like the whole, 'where ya at?' thing. No one likes ending a sentence with a preposition, but we can all learn to live with it and not shoot people."

"I didn't mean to shoot him," said Mr. Willet. "I didn't know the gun had a hair trigger. That is the first time I've ever even shot a gun! I just wanted to make him understand. Make anyone understand the issue with the metal!"

"What about it sir?"

"It is the wrong type of metal!"

"I see your frustration, sir," said the officer. "You were expecting it to say mettle, as in m e t t l e."

"Exactly!" said Mr. Willet, as his face lit up. "You have no idea how wonderful it is to hear you say that. To have someone finally understand what I'm ranting about."

"Yes, sir," said the officer. "I'm a bit of a grammar geek myself. However, it is actually correct."

"What?"

"Well, as the other type of 'mettle' fell out of favor, the colloquial 'metal' took its place. During a good deal of the 17th century both were interchangeable," said the officer. "During most of the 18th and 19th century both were considered correct, and it wasn't until the expulsion of 'mettle' from the vernacular that the other 'metal' actually became correct. Before you kill someone over a billboard, sir you might have wanted to do a bit of research."

A man appeared next to the officer, he was holding a stun gun.

"Take him down," said the officer.

"But," said Mr. Willet, as the dart hit him in the shoulder. "Fuck."

His body jerked onto the pavement, and the news choppers tried to focus in on his body.

Chapter Twenty-Three

Wherein Thomas follows his heart.

"I don't care, I'll do what I want!" said the young woman sitting next to Thomas. The studio audience erupted with cheers. Thomas knew his cue. He prided himself on his professionalism. He stood and walked off stage.

"Wait, Phil!" said the host, as he ran over to Thomas. "Phil, what do you think you're going to do about this?"

"I'll always love my daughter, but I'm not going to watch her throw her life away like this," said Thomas, in a thick southern drawl.

"You ain't my daddy!" screamed the young woman, as she jumped up out of her chair.

"I'm sorry," said Thomas. "I just can't sit by as she makes these horrible choices. I'm done. She's right, she is going to do what she wants, and there ain't nothing I can do about it."

"Look what you've done to your father!" said

the host, Morris Katt.

The studio audience hooted in agreement with the host, and applause roared. Thomas was always impressed how easily a studio audience could be swayed.

"We've all got your back, will you please stay, Phil?" said Morris.

"Let him go," said the young woman. "Fuck him, let him go. I don't care. I'll do what I want!"

The young woman lunged at Thomas. She was quickly intercepted by the host, which changed her balance as well as her trajectory. Her left hand came around and hit Thomas in the eye.

"See," said Thomas, as he walked off the stage.

The back stage crew was quick to congratulate Thomas. He hated doing the shows when they became physical. You never knew the level of professionalism with the people you were working with. The real pros would always rehearse anything physical; the newer kids would just wing it, wanting to make certain that it looked fresh, that it appeared in the moment and not staged. But, that was how you got a black eye and a pissed off host.

"How are you, Thomas?" said Morris, as he rushed backstage.

"I'll be fine, nothing a day or two of rest and some makeup can't take care of," said Thomas.

"Look, you can be assured that that little lady will not be working on my show again anytime soon!"

The young girl who had been playing Thomas' stepdaughter came back stage. Thomas liked her. She was young and sweet, but very green.

"Oh, my God, Thomas," said Gabriella. "Are you okay? It was totally an accident."

"I know," said Thomas. "I don't know why everyone is making such a big deal about it. I'll be fine."

"See, that is a fucking professional," said Morris. "Thomas has been doing the daytime talk show circuit for what? A year now?"

"Yeah," said Thomas.

"And he's played everything from deadbeat dads, to gang members, to abusive husbands, and always the fucking professional," said Morris. "Hell, I know people who've been doing this since before Sally Jessie Raphael went off the air, who aren't as professional as this guy. Thank you Thomas!"

Morris, along with the members of the crew began a slow clap as he walked to his dressing room.

After Mr. Willet's arrest, Thomas tried to return to his life as a TSA agent. However, due to having to keep his relationship with Mr. Willet a secret, he was unable to account for his unscheduled leave, something that his supervisor took little time in pointing out as she showed him the door.

While walking along LaBrea, trying to think of a way to make enough money to finish Mr. Willet's joke, a large U-Haul van pulled up next to him.

A young man in a pinstripe suit lowered the window and said, "Would you like to be on television?"

Thomas looked at the man in the cab of the U-Haul. If he weren't wearing a suit or holding a clipboard he might have ignored him.

"Does it pay anything?"

"Yes, but only if you can make a good

impression during the screening," said the man.

"Sure," said Thomas.

Thomas was quickly shuffled into the back of the U-Haul. Seated on the floor next to other regular looking people. They looked at him as if he knew something about where they were going. He shrugged, and the orange truck sped off.

They were taken to a small studio in the Valley. There were they were assigned roles, and were told to pretend that they were on a talk show. In the center of the studio were a collection of different talk show sets, each placed back to back, so that someone could easily walk the perimeter of the studio and watch scene after scene.

A small group of pretty people in suits entered the studio. As they approached each set, someone would yell action, and the people would have to pretend that they were on a talk show.

Thomas looked across at the barely dressed young woman who was on the set with him.

"Do you mind if I take a swing at you?" said the young woman.

"I guess not," said Thomas. "Am I supposed to be your father?"

"I think so, but if we make it step father it

might give us more to work with," she said. "You can work a bit of the sexual attraction angle, or the replaced father figure? Not that I'm telling you what you should do, I don't want to quarterback this scene."

"Have you done a lot of stuff like this?" said Thomas.

"This is my first gig," she said. "I was doing a lot of rep work in the Midwest, and someone suggested I come out for pilot season. I thought it might be fun."

"Action!" said a voice as the crowd approached the set that Thomas was on.

"I don't care!" said the woman, in a generic Southern accent. "You ain't my, Daddy. I'll do what I want!"

Thomas turned to speak to her, and she swung at him, barely missing his jaw. Thomas pretended that it had connected, staggering back.

"That's it," he said, mimicking her generic Southern accent. "I don't know why you feel the need to hurt me, but I am done being hurt by you. You hear me, done! I want you out."

"What?" said the young lady. "What do you mean out?"

"I'm done with you bitin' the hand that feeds you! You hear me, done! You don't want me to be the boss of you that's fine, I won't be. But, I ain't payin' for shit! You hear me, nothin'!"

"And scene," said the voice from the crowd. "Thank you, if you could both have a seat we'll be with you shortly."

"So where are you from?" said the young lady no longer in her generic Southern accent.

"Originally Eugene, Oregon," said Thomas, "but, I've lived most of my life here in Southern California."

"Wow," she said, "almost a native. I've always thought that we should ask people where they went to high school, rather than where they were born. Where someone is born has more to do with geography. Where someone went to high school has more to do with the society that people were raised in. For example, my boyfriend was born in Germany, but went to high school in Portland, Oregon. So now no matter where he goes everyone assumes he's a hipster. I bet you get that a lot, too."

"Not really," said Thomas. "I don't think anyone has ever confused me with a hipster."

"I don't know. With how cute you are I

wouldn't be surprised."

"Now," said the man in the group. If the two of you would be so kind as to follow me."

"I'm sorry," said Thomas, as he stood up, "did we do something wrong?"

"If you could both follow me, for just a quick moment," he repeated.

Cautiously, Thomas and the young woman rose to follow him. He marched them across the studio floor where other people were pretending to be on various talk shows. They exited down a long hallway that lead to a stairwell that emptied out into a nice suite of offices where a woman was waiting with a clipboard. She smiled broadly when she saw them.

"Hello, Mary and Thomas," said the woman.

"I feel a fool," said Thomas, turning to the young woman. "I never introduced myself, I'm Thomas."

"I'm Mary."

"And the two of you are just magnificent," said the woman with the clipboard. "I've got a proposition for you. However, before that I need you both to sign a non-disclosure agreement."

"Can I guess," said Thomas. "It says we won't

tell anyone that the majority of people who actually appear on these kind of talk shows are actually actors?"

"Unfortunately, I can't say anything until you sign the agreement."

Thomas did. And that was how he found himself backstage of the Morris Katt show, icing down his eye.

Thomas sighed heavily. It had been nearly sixteen months since the heroic efforts of Mr. Willet to bring to the world a new kind of humor. He had given him an envelope to open in the event of him not succeeding. He just couldn't bear it. The thought of opening the envelope meant that Mr. Willet wasn't coming back, even though he knew that the trial didn't go the way that any of them had hoped. At least Mr. Willet was sent to a mental institution, rather than to prison. Mr. Willet's lawyers had been hoping for him to be simply placed in a rehab outpatient facility. But when Mr. Willet was insistent that he wasn't now, nor had he been taking any drugs when he seemingly began his self-described rampage for grammatical purity.

The media quickly grabbed hold of the phrase grammatical purity. They quickly became focused on the word, 'purity,' which caused quite a few people to believe the incident was racially motivated. One expert stated that it must have been Mr. Willet's deep anti-Semitic views that caused him to storm his agent's office. Three anchors got in trouble for assuming that Mr. Willet's agent was Jewish. This did nothing to turn the conversation back towards grammar. Fingers were pointed, and the public was outraged.

Luckily, shortly before sentencing a young starlet was found passed out behind the wheel of a car that plowed into a day care center. Very little attention was placed on the fact that it was at 4am and that the center was empty. But, this momentary distraction was all the judge needed to be able bring back a recommendation for a psychiatric evaluation.

Thomas wanted to visit Mr. Willet in the mental institution, but thought that it might bring him under suspicion. After he found his new job, Thomas rented an apartment in the heart of Koreatown. He paid cash and lived modestly. He placed the envelope from Mr. Willet on a small table. He would occasionally dust it, but it sat there unopened for a very long time.

Thomas would think about what the envelope might contain. He would get drunk and talk to it. On more than one occasion he would throw it in the trash, only to retrieve it the next day.

Today, after he got home from the Morris Katt program, he sat down on his couch and pulled out an e-cigarette. It was bad habit he picked up working the talk show circuit. He took a long pull of the e-cigarette, jumped to his feet, crossed the room and opened the envelope.

Chapter Twenty-Four

The fourth excerpt from <u>Crazy Rhythm</u> by Nicolas
Irons

"Because, it is the right thing to do."

"What is the right thing to do?" said Abigail.

"Sorry," said Anton. "There are times when I
talk to myself. I don't mean to, but for some reason
I carry on entire conversations in my head. I think
it has a lot to do with the amount of time that I
spend alone."

"Well, if you would like you could talk to me,"
said Abigail. "It might make the time go by a bit
quicker."

"It might," said Anton. "There are times that
I am going to need you to be quiet though."

"I understand."

"How are you managing that?"

"Managing what?"

"Walking right now. I mean how is it that you
can actually make it along here without tripping."

"This is where I grew up. I used to play in these woods. Why wouldn't I be able to make my way through."

"It really is very remarkable."

A phonograph could be heard in the distance.

"Do you hear it as well?" he said.

"Yes," said Abigail. "I'm not certain if I should be excited or frightened. What do you think Anton?"

"I don't know," said Anton. "That is why I am going to have to ask you to stay here for a moment."

"No, please don't leave me here," said Abigail.

"I'm just going to go and make certain that it is safe," he said. "Whatever it is, it's making a hell of a racket. If it doesn't stop, we're going to have everyone in a five-mile radius on top of us. I will be back as soon as I can, I promise."

"Please don't," said Abigail.

Anton ignored her plea and set of swiftly toward the sound of the opera in the distance. Once he was far enough away, he began slowing down to see what was ahead. Before him, in a small clearing, were the bodies of six soldiers. Anton recognized the music as an early aria from Mozart's "The Marriage of Figaro".

"This was always my favorite," said his Grandmother's voice. "Do you remember when I took you to see it?"

"Yes," said Anton. "But, could you hold that thought for just a moment? I need to see what's going on here, and can't be taking the time to go back with you right now."

"Well, if that's the way that you're going to be about it," she said.

"I don't mean to be rude, Grandma," said Anton. "But, I'm really very scared right now."

"As well you should be," said the soldier in front of him. He was dressed in a uniform that Anton didn't recognize. He was holding a long knife and smiling. "You should be completely terrified. If you weren't I would suspect that there might be something really very wrong with you. Here you are in the middle of a strange wood, with a strange woman, and you don't know where you're going or how in the world you're going to find your way back out. Someone is blasting opera, and you're not sure if you are going to have enough food to make it through. Am I right?"

"Yes."

"But, you don't have anything to worry

about, that is if you are American, or at least not German," said the soldier. "You aren't are you?"

"No," said Anton. "I'm Belgian."

"Wearing and American uniform?" said the soldier. "That makes me very happy, you escaped?"

"Not yet," said Anton.

"I like you," said the soldier. "I am here trying to kill as many of them as I can, please let me show you." The soldier led him behind a small tent where there were sixteen bodies all stacked on top of each other.

"I will have to do something when the thaw comes," said the soldier. "But, then I might not be here at that time. But, then I might. The way things are going you never know what is going to happen, do you?"

"No, you don't," said Anton.

"And that is what is scaring the hell out of you right now isn't it?"

"Yes."

"Then tell me why don't you run?" said the soldier.

"I can't."

"Oh, I'm certain that I could make you run if

you needed to."

"The boots, don't fit," said Anton. "Anything other than a steady march and I'll trip over myself."

"And the girl," said the soldier. "You haven't mentioned the girl, have you? Why not? Something wrong with her?"

"Please leave her alone."

"Why?" said the soldier. "Why the hell should I even think about leaving either of you alone. For all I know you are both lying to me."

"You haven't even spoken to her."

"Shut up! Shut up! Shut up! I'm in charge here. Don't you understand that? I've got a pile of bodies, dirty evil bodies; I've seen what they've done. I've seen how they starve people out. I've watched people catch and eat rats, just so their children don't go hungry. And I'm not going anywhere until I kill every last one of these bastards for a five mile radius."

The phonograph began to wind down. The soldier walked over to it and gave it a good crank. Anton picked up the rock silently.

"I could easily say that you were both German, just add you to the pile. I'd bet you those shoes would fit me a good deal better than they do you? And the girl, who's to say she needs to go quickly? If she is a little German slut who's to say I shouldn't have a little fun-"

The soldier didn't have a chance to finish his sentence. Anton brought the heavy rock down hard on the back of his head. He kept hitting it over and over again. The blood splattered on his hands. It was almost like the blood was flowing out of his head onto the rock and up his wrists.

"Anton?" said Abigail, as she came around the side of the tent. "Is there someone else here? I heard a voice."

"There was someone, but they're gone now," said Anton.

"Oh, why did they leave?" she said.

Anton began wiping his hands across the white snow, leaving wild patterns of red troughs. Drying them on the damp burlap caused the blood to pool and drip down he side of the tent, landing in the muddy divots left by his boots. Anton looked down at how huge the footprint was. He thought about how much blood would have to run down the side of the tent, avoiding the small divots and irregularities in the fabric to finally fill the footprint.

"Be thankful they did," said Anton. "He was a bit off."

"In what way?" she said.

"Look, we really need to not dawdle," said Anton. "It looks like it is going to start snowing again at any minute. Let's get to the next village and see about holing up for the night."

An aria came to a close and the record stopped. The muffled silence of the snow made the world suddenly feel very small, insulated. Like it was stuffed in cotton.

"Let's go," said Abigail.

Anton turned the corner to see a second pile of bodies. A pile of much smaller bodies than the one he had been looking at earlier.

"What is it?" said Abigail. "What's wrong?"

"Why does there have to be something wrong?" said Anton.

"Because, there has been for so very long," said Abigail.

Anton looked deep into the milky dead eye of a young boy. He looked to be about seven. His skin was grey.

"There's a small yellow flower, and it's just beginning to poke it's way through the snow," said Anton. "Just don't want us to step on it. It's beautiful, and very delicate. So, I just want you to walk this way a bit more, and then we can continue."

"That's wonderful, possibly the first sign of spring?" said Abigail.

"Just a little bit of hope," said Anton.

"Or it could just be a flower that will die off with the next hard frost," said his wife's voice.

"Why do you have to be like this," he said, turning to her. She was sitting on the hard wooden chair shivering from the cold. She had a quilt tight around her. Her color looked off. He knew she was very sick.

"Like what?" she said. "Do you like always having your head in the clouds? Why don't you come down here and be with me. That's all I need right now. I don't need promises of things getting better, or spring, or warmth. I don't need you to make this right, I just need you to come and be."

"I can't right now," he said.

"Why not?" she said.

"Right now I have too much that I need to do. I have to much that needs to be set right."

"You don't need to fix this. I'm not sure you can. You can hardly stand up straight in boots that don't come anywhere near close to fitting."

"I need to do this," said Anton.

"It won't bring any of it back," she said. "You do understand that don't you?"

"Please, just leave me alone," said Anton.

"I don't want to be a nuisance," said Abigail. "You're the one who had them take my brother."

"I'm sorry I was thinking out loud again," said Anton. He looked around to see hat he had led her to the edge of a quiet village. It looked like the one they had just left.

"You should stop doing that if you want to keep friends," said Abigail.

"So, we're friends now?"

"Don't know. I haven't decided, yet."

Anton smiled at her.

"I'm smiling at you," he said. "What is the nearest village to yours?"

"There is one to the East, another to the West," she said. "But, the one to the West is close to the border. The truck drove off to the East."

"Yes, but they are doubling back," he said. "As long as we're heading to the West everything is going to be just fine. Do you know this village well?"

"A little, there was a small cafe my father took me to here once," said Abigail. "I remember it well because there was a stair case down to the cafe, and they were playing jazz."

"It doesn't sound much like a cafe, it sounds more like a bar," said Anton. "Not that I have a problem with a bar, especially not if we're going to hole up for the night."

"Do you think it might be better to find a place with a bed?"

"I don't know how deserted this place is, but if you came home and found someone sleeping in your bed, how shocked would you be? Would you chase Goldilocks out, or ask her if she wanted to stay?"

"The cafe was two blocks up on the South side of the street, the stairs are around a corner."

Anton led Abigail onto the muddy lane, and began walking toward the cafe. The street was abandoned except for the occasional body. They walked through the mud, and down the stone stairs into the basement cafe.

Anton forced the door open with his shoulder. The tables and chairs were set up as if the cafe was prepared for the next sitting. Anton looked around to see if they were truly alone. A thorough inspection of what was once the kitchen, revealed that there was no one there, but there was a good deal of wine and hard liquor.

"Well, there doesn't seem to be much to eat, but there is plenty to drink," said Anton. "And it looked like you were right, it appears we do have some jazz music. Do you have any preference?"

"I would very muck like a glass of wine and some music, sir," she said.

Anton placed a record onto the phonograph, and a loud clarinet shrieked out of it.

"Crazy Rhythm!" said Abigail. "My favorite!"

Anton smiled at the sound. He pulled a bottle of wine from the rack and using a clumsy looking opener, somehow got the bottle open.

"Are you really sure that this is what you should do?" said his grandmother's voice. "You don't even know if that little thing there is old enough to drink."

"Are you old enough to drink," called Anton.

"Yes," said Abigail.

"There you are," he said under his breath. "I just want to have a nice relaxing evening. I'm not saying I want to get drunk. I'm not saying I want to get her drunk. All I'm saying is that I want her to relax. I want to relax. I want to take a minute to breathe. Is that really such a horrible thing?"

"You don't have enough bad luck, you have to go looking for it now?"

Anton placed a glass in front of Abigail. He gently placed her hand on the glass. She took a sip and smiled. Anton took a long pull from the bottle.

The door to the cafe creaked open slowly to reveal a soldier in a beige uniform with a red armband.

He was badly injured, and could barely stand. Anton wasn't certain if he had even noticed them. He staggered in to the cafe, and looked straight at Anton. Anton stared back in silence. Abigail took another sip of the wine.

"This is very good," she said. "Do you think we might be able to start a small fire to get warm and dry? I am looking forward to being warm and dry."

The soldier took out his pistol and aimed it directly at Abigail. Anton quickly moved between Abigail and the soldier. The soldier pulled the trigger. Anton waited for the bang that never happened. The soldier pulled the trigger another time, and another, and another. Finally he looked at the empty gun and collapsed onto a table, crashing chairs.

"What was that?" asked Abigail.

"If we're going to have a fire, we're going to need fire wood aren't we," said Anton. "I just thought a few of these chairs would make a good start. But, I think it would be better if I were to step out quickly and see what we might have outside. Will you be okay here by yourself?"

"Just leave the wine bottle and I'll be just fine."

Anton dragged the body of the soldier out into the muddy street. The soldier groggily reached around for something to stop him being dragged back out into the cold. He dug his hand into the frozen mud of the lane. Anton tried to get him to a more discreet location. But, he was beginning to fight more than Anton was ready to deal with. He rolled the body of the soldier over and grasped his neck with both hands, and began to squeeze, tighter and tighter. The soldier continued to flail for another moment, until he abruptly stopped.

"Really?" said his wife's voice. "Did that really need to happen?"

"Look, I'm about at the edge of reason at this moment and I really don't want to do this right now," said Anton.

"And when do you think a better time might be?" said his grandmother's voice. "When you end up with that poor girl dead?"

"That poor girl?" said Anton. "What the hell are you talking about with that poor girl, and the rest of this damned nonsense? What the hell, I'm just trying to get to the border. I'm just trying to go home, that is all I want, to go home."

"Then go," said Hans. "I don't know what the hell is keeping you here! That little German thing in there? How easy did she have it? How many times did you have to suffer while she was sitting with her friends, and maybe her brother? What the hell? Just leave!"

"No," said Anton. "I'm not going to and there is nothing any of you can say that is going to change my mind. I am going to take that poor scared little girl with me."

"You're a liar," said his Grandmother.

"And you're scaring me," said his son.

"Why don't you all just go away? Why don't you see about leaving me in peace? I don't want any of you here, do you understand me? Why don't you all just go away!"

The snow was crisply on the frozen street. It sounded like someone dropping small shards of glass onto a window.

"I said did you hear me?!" continued Anton. He looked around in rage at the street. The sound of the snow falling was all that answered back.

Abigail was standing in the middle of the street.

"Hello?" said Anton, realizing exactly how small he felt.

"Hello," said Abigail. "Would you like to come back inside?"

"Certainly," said Anton, as he rushed at her savagely. "Why not? We can make a party out of it! Shall we?"

"Anton?" she said, as he pulled her into the small cafe.

"No," said Anton. "I don't want to talk anymore. All I want to do now is start a small fire and drink. Maybe I'll eat some chocolate. But I am going to sit here and get very drunk."

"Are you sure that is wise?" said Abigail.

"What would you know about being wise?" said Anton. "How old are you? Sixteen? Seventeen? What do you know about being wise? All I ever see from you is you needing. Why the hell are you always so needy?"

"What do you mean 'always'?" said Abigail. "You just met me. Who the hell are you to tell me what I should or shouldn't say? What is the high cost for your misguided generosity? Should we bow before you as our great liberator?"

Anton thought about speaking, but simply placed the bottle of wine to his lips, and broke another chair, then another, and another.

Abigail ran to the door and out into the night. Anton thought about breaking another chair. He placed the bottle down and then ran out after her. He thought of the nightmare world waiting for her outside.

Abigail was walking along slowly trying to feel her way. Anton smiled for a quick moment.

She looked like a small child learning to walk, holding onto a table, or the pant leg of a parent.

The burst of gunfire came quickly and her body fell quietly onto the muddy street. Anton fought the urge to run to her, and tried to see where the shooter had been. Looking up into the windows across the street, Anton saw a figure move from the window. Terrified that he might be spotted, Anton snuck back into the shadow and waited.

"You need to make yourself as tiny as you can, Daddy," said his son's voice. "As tiny as your body will let you. You need to think of your self as not even there, do you understand, Daddy?"

Anton nodded his head, afraid to make a noise. He looked out at the street waiting for the figure to appear and examine the body. He tried to calm his breathing in the quiet lane. His heart pounded. He knew he was going to be found.

"Calm down, Daddy," said his son's voice. "It's going to be okay. Just stay where you are and everything will be okay."

Anton thought about taking his eyes off the body in the middle of the street. Maybe, if he turned around, his son might be there. He might be able to grab him and hold him as tightly as he could manage. That wouldn't really be the worst way to go, would it? He could just stand up and turn his back on the shooter, hold his son, and receive a bullet to the head. That could be the end.

He turned and closed his eyes. He hoped that when he opened them he would be in their apartment. He could just walk into he bedroom and grab his son, and be with them all again. He opened his eyes, and was still standing on the street.

"Why?" said Anton. "Why is it that sometimes it works and other times it doesn't? Is there some kind of rule that I'm not following? I don't understand this!"

Anton turned back around to see a soldier standing in the middle of the street. He had his rifle trained on Anton.

The soldier's uniform looked different, not American, not German, something different. It took Anton a moment, but then saw that he was a Soviet. Anton smiled and stepped toward him, and the man pulled the trigger on the rifle. There was the sound of a click, then the sound of another click. The soldier turned and began running in the opposite direction.

"Wait!" said Anton. "Please."

The soldier stopped in the snowy street.

"Why?" said the soldier.

"Because, I would like to talk to you," said Anton. "If only for a moment."

"Why?" said the soldier. "Why would you want to talk? I think there has been enough talking so far. There has been nothing but talk to get us into this."

"Would you kill me?" said Anton. "Please?"

"I am out of bullets," said the soldier.

"Then don't use bullets," said Anton.

"I can't," said the soldier. "I'm not strong enough."

"You don't know," said Anton. "I am very weak."

"You will fight back," said the soldier.

"No, I won't."

"You don't think you will, but you will fight back," said the soldier. "Everyone does, no matter how hopeless it all feels. No matter how close you feel you are to the end. You may think you are prepared, and I'm certain you probably are. Here you are talking to me when I just killed the girl you were with. What was she to you, a friend?"

"Just someone I was trying to help," said

Anton.

"So, now you feel that there is nothing left?" said the soldier. "You can't help the young girl, how can you help yourself? That will carry you through the beginning. You will lie down on the cold ground, and you will let me wrap my hands around your neck. You will let me squeeze, but as you struggle for a breath and close your eyes, something happens. Your brain will spark, and soon you will fight me. You will claw at my face, trying to break my hold. You will succeed. I am not strong enough. If I had more bullets, you would be dead already. How ironic? The one time I find someone who wants to die, and I'm out of ammunition."

"What should I do now?"

"What do you think you should do now?" said the soldier. "You've gotten yourself this far. You've seen the retreat of the convoys. Your troops will be coming along any moment, and then what."

"They aren't my troops," said Anton. "I found the uniform."

"Do you think they'll care?" said the soldier. "They're just going to see that uniform. even if you pretend to be mute, they'll take care of you. You'll be given a warm bed, and if you were smart enough to take the poor bastard's dog tags with you when you took the clothes, they may even ship you off to the States. Don't be a fool. You have too much to gain by just keeping your mouth shut."

"But, the boots don't fit," said Anton.

"Trust me, when it comes to this, no one's boots fit."

"So, what do I do now?"

"Why are you asking me?" said the soldier.

Anton launched himself at the soldier with a ferocity that surprised even Anton.

The soldier turned and ran.

Anton landed in the muddy street.

"You're staring to pick up a few bad habits," said Hans's voice. "I would have to say that I blame the Germans. Not the cute little one you've been hanging out with, but the rest of them. Yes, you've picked up a few bad habits."

"I wanted to kill him," said Anton.

"Of course you did," said Hans. "He killed your only chance at redemption, didn't he? Out of the people you've killed in the past forty-eight hours, I would say that he was the one who really deserved it. He was also planning on killing you.

But, that doesn't mean that it is okay to keep killing people."

"I don't know why everything keeps going wrong," said Anton.

"What do you mean going wrong?" said Hans. "For you lately everything has been going well. You're alive, aren't you? That has to count for something. You survived, and you're continuing to. You were cold, you found dry clothes. You were hungry you found chocolate. Chocolate! How much to you need, Anton? Please, tell me how much do you need to feel that things are starting to turn around for you? Do you want a bunch of call girls to fall out of the sky onto your penis? You were enjoying a bit of wine and some jazz."

"And I was almost killed."

"True, but that is the start of a great day."

"Having someone almost kill you should be the highlight of my day?"

"It's the almost part that I am trying to emphasize," said Hans. "You need to start taking stock and seeing what is going on here."

Anton sat down on the cold ground. He looked over at the pool of blood in which Abigail's body was laying. The red ran into the divots in the road, settling into deep crimson pools. The warmth of the blood melted the snow around, mixing with it, watering down the severity of the color. Anton looked up as the snow was falling again. The flakes were becoming larger, less frozen and more the kind of snow that you find in the movies. Beautiful imaginary snow, in a beautiful imaginary world. A perfect silver world, where after the curtain falls, the actors who had been shot would stand up to go and work another day.

Anton thought about the last time he had seen a movie. He knew it had to have been one with Uncle Hans in it. He sat in the velvet seat. His son hadn't been able to come, which worked well for Anton's wife. She loved Uncle Hans, but hadn't much cared for his last film. She always wondered why he played such buffoons. Why couldn't he play something a bit truer to his character?

Anton sat in the darkened theater, and the newsreel finished, and the film began. As it did he saw Uncle Hans being chased through the street. He was sweaty and disheveled. The camera came in close to his face, and he could see the desperation in his eyes. The rest of the audience, tittered for a moment, not certain what this comedian was doing. There hadn't been a prat fall, or a single attractive woman for him to leer at.

As the film went on, Anton found himself transported into this dark eerie world, which the film inhabited. It told the story of a child murderer, and his need to escape from being caught. It was nothing like anything Uncle Hans had ever made before. A few of the audience members rose to leave. The images in the film were too dark.

"I though it was going to be the greatest movie I would ever make," said Hans.

"I like it," said Anton.

"Yes, but no one else did," said Hans. "I thought this was going to be the one, the one that I would be able to go to Hollywood on. Just goes to show you."

"Well, are you happy with your performance?"

"Yes," said Uncle Hans. "But, don't be naive. I'm only ever as good as the audience decides. That is the reality behind what we do. That is what happens when you create."

Anton looked up at the dark sky as the snow began to swirl around and make new patterns. He smiled as the snow hit his face and melted.

Anton turned to Nicolas and said, "You realize that this isn't really much of and ending, don't you?"

Nicolas looked around at the snowy street.

"I am talking to you," said Anton.

"What is going on?" said Nicolas. "Where am I?"

"You're in a coma," said Anton. "Don't worry you'll be waking up shortly. This isn't an ending. I mean, we haven't resolved anything. I've killed more people than in an 80's action movie, teetering on the edge of madness for the past hundred and fifty pages. Then you kill off Abigail, really just for shock value, and have me hallucinate that I'm in a movie theatre. WTF?"

Nicolas looked off into the hills, a plume of dark smoke rose from a spot not far from them.

"There's a fire," said Nicolas.

"Who cares?" said Anton. "Why didn't you just kill me off?"

"You can't just arbitrarily kill off characters," said Nicolas. "If you're going to kill someone off, you have to have a reason."

"Then why did you kill everyone else off?"

"To show how brutal life can be," said Nicolas

"Oh," said Anton. "So, killing me off would somehow not show how brutal it could be? Or, having me find my way to liberation?"

"I didn't want a predictable ending."

"So, you decided to just not have one."

"Fuck you," said Nicolas, as he woke up.

Last Thursday

Chapter Twenty-Five

Wherein Nicolas wakes up.

The light hurt his eyes. Why the hell would anyone place a light right where he was trying to look, thought Nicolas. There were noises, which were loud and annoying, but they were nothing compared with the light. It made his head pound to look at it. Somewhere to his left a man sniffed. It startled him. He didn't expect to jump but he did. A young nurse came over.

"Doctor?" yelled the young man.

Nicolas wondered why was a doctor here. Who the hell was calling for a doctor? Where the hell was he? Nicolas tried to sit up.

"We need a doctor over here right now!"

Christina had been on set for the majority of the afternoon, her cell phone turned off. Walking to her car was the first she had heard about Nicolas waking up.

"You have got to have the most amazing fucking timing I think I have ever heard!" said Christina, as she hugged Nicolas.

"Why?" asked Nicolas. "You don't want to say anything about how you're happy that I woke up from a fucking coma?"

"Yeah, that really is a great thing!" said Christina. "But, the movie premieres next week."

"What movie?"

"Your movie," said Christina. "This is fucking amazing. Once word gets out that you're up! The press! Can you even wrap your mind around the fucking press!"

"I'm really fucking confused here," said Nicolas.

"We made the movie," said Christina. "We made Crazy Rhythm! After the story came out, about how you were shot."

"Shot?"

"Do you remember being in Tyler's office?" said Nicolas.

"There was the guy in the suit?"

"Yeah," said Christina. "Come to find out, it

was Mr. Willet."

"The self-proclaimed king of late night?"

"Yeah, I guess he didn't mean to shoot you," said Christina. "It was some weird racist, anti-Semitic, sexist thing. Who really gives a fuck? He was a whack job."

"Well, of course he was. He shot me."

"But, that was the kicker," said Christina. "He didn't mean to actually kill anyone. It was supposed to be some kind of a punch line to some kind of an elaborate joke that no one understood. I mean the guy just went loopy, went to Japan, and came back even loopier."

"Wow," said Nicolas. "But, what does this have to do with anything?"

"Once the story got out about you being this young novelist, coming to Los Angeles to sell the rights to your book, everyone wanted to help. Tyler and Saul weren't even pissed that you signed another deal. They just wanted to ensure that your vision made it to the screen."

"Really?"

"They weren't the only ones. People volunteered to help make this movie. From the cast to the crew, they all signed on, and made sure that what little fees they were given were instead put towards your care in the hospital. They even signed over their percentages of the film to you, so if you ever woke up, you would have something to live off of. As of this moment you actually own over 85% of a movie that is opening worldwide next week. Even if the movie flops you will be a very rich man, and this doesn't include how your book has been selling! With you awake and able to attend the opening, this is going to be absolutely huge!"

"Wow," said Nicolas. "I guess I'm kind of speechless. I didn't realize that this was something that could happen."

"What, you thought that everyone out here was just in this for the money?" said Christina. "There is no need to be rude. There are a few of us out here that are into this for the art, the beautiful process of creation, elevating a piece of art to something else."

"Which was why you had me meeting with pornographers."

"Don't be so judgmental," said Christina.

Chapter Twenty-Six

Wherein Thomas goes on a West Encino adventure.

Thomas looked at the brochure. A very tan man with a bright smile was on the front. In large Papyrus typeface were the words, "You might achieve your dreams alone. But, with Dr. Orga's help, you may achieve them faster!"

Thomas assumed the man on the front of the brochure was Dr. Orga. He tried to understand why Mr. Willet would have left him a brochure for a self-help seminar, which took place in Calabasas over a year ago? On the inside, still in the Papyrus font, were inspirational quotes, as well as a website where one could pre-register.

Thomas found the website which had the same offensive font. An image of the man sat there, his pixels burning into the screen. It didn't take long for him to register for his next seminar, which was taking place at the West Encino Community Center.

There was nothing offensive regarding the Community Center. It had been purposely designed in a way to not offend anyone, and therefore could not be deemed endearing by anyone either. The orange tile roof was making a valiant effort trying to look authentic, as was the peeling sun bleached once beige stucco.

Thomas stood in front of the Community Center. There was just so much Papyrus font that Thomas felt a little bit of his soul fading into non-existence. A steady flow of people, many of them looking like they were desperate for an answer, entered the building, all of them were willing to pay, all of them willing to sit and listen to hear what the tan man had to say: in the misguided hope that this lone man presenting at the West Encino Community Center might hold the key to their happiness and success. Thomas joined the crowd that was searching the registration desk for their nametags and registration materials. The table was divided between general, bronze, silver gold, platinum, VIP and VIP+.

Thomas found his badge with the general admission pile and followed the crowd into the auditorium, where each tier had been segregated. Underpaid ushers lazily showed people to the general area of their seats.

Even when Thomas ignored the directions of the ushers and went to sit in the VIP+ section, they didn't seem to care. It was clearly an issue that someone of a higher pay grade could deal with.

The lights dimmed. An inspirational and uplifting guitar riff blasted through the large speakers on the side of the stage. Somewhere behind a large plastic fern a fog machine started.

The uneven fog drifted into the VIP section, but not the VIP+ section. The attendees who were stuck in the VIP section choking on the pretend fog thought about moving to the neighboring VIP+ section. But, instead of moving, they sat in their assigned seats blaming themselves for not shelling out the extra money to sit in the VIP+ section.

Thomas noticed a few people sitting in the "platinum" section who were giggling at the people who were stuck in the fog. A distorted voice came over the speakers. The speaker was both speaking too loudly and holding the microphone too close to his mouth.

A man emerged with a comb-over and a bad

spray tan. Instead of making him look healthy, it actually made him look jaundiced. He flashed a bluish smile. Thomas knew it was a side effect of some of the cheaper tooth whiteners. He vaguely resembled Dr. Orga from the brochure.

"Ladies and Gentlemen, are you ready to change your life?" said Dr. Orga. He meant it to sound like a definitive statement, something to rile up the crowd. Sadly it came out as more of a question than anything else. The crowd however, desperate to hear anything that could help make sense of their lives, applauded. Including those in the VIP section who were still choking on the fake fog.

"I hope so!" continued Dr. Orga. "Because, today is the day where everything changes, for you, and you, and also you." He stopped and pointed directly at Thomas. Thomas smiled at the man on stage. "And right now I am going to start with our VIP+ member! While I have one of my colleagues talk to you for a short while, I am going to speak with the lone VIP+ member, giving him my undivided attention for a sold fifteen minutes. For those of you who would like the same, it isn't too late! Head on out into the lobby and let them know that you would like to upgrade to VIP+, right now! And for those of you who cannot afford it, don't worry, much of what is discussed privately will be imparted to you as well. Although not quite as targeted as this gentleman is going to receive, but there is still time! Sir, if you would like to follow me."

Dr. Orga walked off stage, Thomas followed. As he disappeared, an attractive woman took the stage.

"Are you ready to be free?" said the woman.

Thomas followed the man down a corridor.

"What is your name?" said Dr. Orga.

"Thomas Sourwood, sir," said Thomas.

Dr. Orga turned to an attractive woman who had joined them as they walked down the hallway, "Mary? Why didn't Thomas here make the list? If I've said it once I've said it a thousand fucking times, when we have a VIP+ member sign up, I want to know it right away!"

"Yes, sir," said Mary.

Dr. Orga made a sharp turn into the restroom.

Thomas and Mary stopped outside.

"Well, go on," said Mary.

"I'm sure he'll only be a minute," said Thomas.

"No, he wants you to go in," said Mary.

"Really?"

"Trust me I've been his personal assistant for years," said Mary. "This is where he does some of his best work."

Thomas cautiously poked his head into the restroom.

"Hello?" he said

"So," said Dr. Orga. "Are you ready to change your life?"

"I guess," said Thomas, as he entered the bathroom.

"Let me guess," said Dr. Orga. "You don't particularly like your job, do you?"

"Not really," said Thomas

"Can you think back to a time when you did?"

"Sure."

"Can you tell me about the job?"

"Well," said Thomas. "I was working for this person-"

"Stop right there," said Dr. Orga. "Was it the job or the person who makes your face light up like this?"

"Both."

"And can you work for this person anymore?"

"No."

"Gone out of business?"

"Kind of," said Thomas.

"Was it his vision or his tactics?" said Dr. Orga. "Most ventures fail, either due to a lack of vision, or a failure in tactics."

"I'm not certain."

"You sure as shit better get certain, because the way that you answer that question will determine your course from here on out. You've been on a path that is not leading you to where you want to go. So why not change course. Look back at when you were happy. Fulfill the vision of your former mentor, without the tactical errors, or if the vision was faulty, apply the tactics he or she used to the next chapter of your life."

"May I be frank with you?" said Thomas.

"Of course you can, if you can be frank in three minutes or less, other folks are waiting."

"I wasn't expecting you to actually help," said Thomas.

Overwhelmed, Thomas turned to give Dr. Orga a hug. Startled, Dr. Orga stepped backwards.

He slipped on a wet spot on the floor. Tumbling backwards he slammed his head on the side of a urinal, bounced off, and landed on the floor with a sharp crack.

Thomas watched as Dr. Orga's head slowly became surrounded by an ever-expanding halo of blood.

Chapter Twenty-Seven

Wherein Nicolas takes a trip to West Encino.

"I don't know if I want the first time I see it to be the premier," said Nicolas.

"Don't be difficult," said Christina, as she swerved around the large red bus that came to an abrupt stop in front of them. "Why the hell wouldn't you want to go?"

"I'm not saying that I don't want to go to the premiere," said Nicolas. "What I'm saying is that I'm not sure I want that to be the first time I see it. Especially if I'm going to have to sell it."

"Then I guess I'm the greatest fucking manager you've ever met!"

"What do you mean?"

"Do you think we're driving all the fuck out to West Encino to go for a burger?"

"I don't know," said Nicolas. "I've never been to West Encino."

"The production company rented out a

theatre," said Christina. "Just a little something they wanted to do for you. That's the way this has all gone down. It's remarkable how everyone has come together for this production. It is just beautiful."

"Really?" said Nicolas.

"Look," said Christina, "there is a long line of people who are going to be there and every one of them want to thank you."

"For?"

"Writing such an amazing book."

Christina pulled the SUV into the parking lot of a generic strip mall. In the center was a generic movie theatre, outside of which stood a long line of people. When they spotted the SUV they all began to applaud. The applause grew louder as Nicolas emerged from the car. Christina helped him into the waiting wheelchair. More than a few of the faces were familiar to Nicolas. Some could have been considered actual movie stars. Nicolas was impressed, and somewhat humbled.

Bruce Prise walked out from the line and held out his hand to Nicolas.

"Mr. Irons, sir," he said, in a thick Australian accent. "I am truly humbled. It is quite an honor to meet you. Your novel changed my life."

"And you changed mine," said Nicolas. The crowd around them laughed warmly.

"Would it be okay if I were to assist you into the theatre?" said Bruce.

"Sure," said Nicolas.

The theatre was what one might find in any suburban strip mall. Bruce wheeled Nicolas to one of the spots designated to accommodate someone in a wheelchair.

"Can I get you anything, sir?" said Bruce.

"No, thanks," said Nicolas.

Bruce blushed and went to sit next to his supermodel girlfriend.

"What do you think?" said Christina, as she took the seat next to Nicolas.

"It is an awful lot to digest," said Nicolas.

"This movie meant a lot to a whole bunch of people," she said.

The lights dimmed. Logos of various production companies flashed across the screen. Finally, they stopped and the words Crazy Rhythm came into focus on the screen, and then transitioned into a brutal looking landscape. A man, who Nicolas assumed was Anton, staggered over the rough snowy terrain.

Anton took a deep breath and began to sing.

"What the fuck was that?" said Nicolas, as he wheeled himself out of the theatre.

"Please don't do this here," said Christina.

"Why the hell shouldn't I do this here?" said Nicolas. "What the fuck did you do?"

"What do you mean?" said Christina. "We made your book into a movie."

"Why did you ruin it?"

"What?"

"You made it a fucking musical!"

"So what?" said Christina. "You didn't want us to change the name, so we didn't. You didn't want us to take out the Nazis, so we didn't. You didn't want us to fuck with the ending, so we didn't. You never once said a god damned thing about not turning it into a musical"

"Is everything okay?" said Bruce, as he came out of the theatre. "I'm about to have my cameo."

"Your what?" said Nicolas.

"I play the body in the tree," said Bruce.

"You have got to be fucking kidding me!" said

Nicolas, as he angrily wheeled himself out the sliding doors of the movie theatre.

"Nicolas!" said Christina, as she followed him out into the parking lot. "You have to see the whole thing to understand. Some of Uncle Hans' songs are so haunting! He has a whole number with the Hitler marionette, in a minor key. Did you hear, a minor key!"

Other people began filing out of the theatre to see what was going on. Nicolas wheeled himself out into the parking lot.

"Please come back, Nick!" said Christina. "There's been Oscar buzz! Suggestions for a Grammy nomination for the soundtrack! Even talk of a Broadway adaptation!"

Nicolas stopped in the fire lane, turned back to the crowd in front of the theatre and said, "Broadway?"

Thomas' car hit Nicolas. The wheelchair, with Nicolas in it, floated above the pavement for what felt to Nicolas like a very long time. In that moment of weightlessness before returning to earth, Nicolas tried to take a deep breath, but his broken ribs would not allow it. He hit the pavement with a loud crack. The wheelchair landed a few feet from him and bounced.

If Thomas hadn't been in such a rush, he would have been interested to note that as Nicolas' blood mixed with the thick valley dust, it increased it's viscosity; impeding its spread across the blacktop.

www.ingramcontent.com/pod-product-compliance
Lightning Source LLC
Chambersburg PA
CBHW021512240626
47154CB00002B/607